DAUGHTERS OF CRUELTY

L.J. DOUGHERTY

Also By L.J. Dougherty

Beasts of the Caliber Lodge

Primal Reserve

Blood Opus

Woodhaven

For Meloy,
Thank you for sitting beside me while I
wrote this book, and all those that preceded it.
You're the best boy.

INTRODUCTION
BY DAVID SODERGREN

Ah, the giallo; that distinctly Italian film genre which blends sex, violence, and high style into a potent brew that is simply irresistible to most fans of cult cinema. It's a genre that is frequently misunderstood — in recent years, any film with colored lights and gels seems to be dubbed a giallo — but what we can surely agree on is that a giallo requires three things; a murder, a mystery, and someone to solve it.

The origins of the term stretch back to 1929, when the Italian publisher Mondadori first released a string of crime and mystery novels in distinctive yellow covers. Giallo is Italian for yellow, and so 'giallo' became a catch-all term for the thriller genre in Italy.

Back then, the books were translations of classic mysteries by the likes of Agatha Christie and Arthur Conan Doyle, a far cry indeed from the lurid pulp of the sexy Italian cinematic thrillers of the sixties and seventies.

In fact, the giallo as we now know it didn't really begin until 1963, with Mario Bava's *The Girl Who Knew Too Much*. This black-and-white mystery introduced several classic tropes, including the American tourist who arrives in Italy and immediately finds themselves embroiled in intrigue, something which may or may not appear in the book you're about to read.

The giallo exploded in popularity in the early seventies, with much of the credit going to Dario Argento, whose debut film — the thrilling mystery *The Bird with the Crystal Plumage* — was an international hit. Hundreds of films followed over the ensuing decade, from the classy (Fulci's *Don't Torture a Duckling* and Luigi Bazzoni's *The Fifth Cord*) to the downright sleazy (Andrea Bianchi's *Strip Nude for Your Killer* and Mario Landi's *Giallo in Venice*). Many followed a similar template, that of the amateur detective who witnesses a murder and takes it upon themselves to track down the killer, usually while all the beautiful people around them fall victim to the murderer, often while in a state of undress.

It's a formulaic genre, but like I told myself when writing my own Scottish giallo, *Dead Girl Blues*, it's not about the story, it's about how you *tell* it.

And that is what's so great about L.J.'s *Daughters Of Cruelty*. If you've read L.J.'s work before — and if you haven't, you should — you'll know he's a fiendishly talented writer with a knack for putting a new twist on an old genre. His trilogy of espionage horror books combined Bond-style spy hi-jinks with fifties monster movies to wonderful effect, and that same skill is strongly in evidence here.

Daughters Of Cruelty hits all the giallo beats — the sex, the violence, the fashion, the mystery — while keeping things fresh with the introduction of several subplots and micro-genres I won't spoil here. It's an homage without being a slavish imitation, and far truer to the spirit of the giallo than any bog-standard slasher with flashing red and blue lights trying to pass itself off as some glorious return to the heyday of Umberto Lenzi and Sergio Martino.

When I read this book, I reached the feverish climax, took a moment to catch my breath, and immediately watched a couple of my favorite gialli, because L.J. reminded me precisely why I love this delirious genre so much. And really, I can't think of a higher compliment than that.

Enjoy the book, and if you ever find yourself vacationing in Italy, watch out for those leather-gloved razor murderers. They're *everywhere*.

David Sodergren
Author of *The Haar, Maggie's Grave,* and *Dead Girl Blues*

DAUGHTERS OF CRUELTY

Chapter 1
Lucia's Last Night In Sicily

Taormina, Sicily.

THE EVENING LUCIA TRANQUILLI was attacked in the presumed safety of her family beach house began pleasantly enough. Her husband's brother, Henri, and his wife, Carrol, had come from Vienna to visit — an annual reunion of the two couples that had begun several years prior after the brothers had moved several cities apart. The beach house had become their rendezvous point. An oasis getaway from their busy lives.

While it was not the only beach house in the area, an extensive stretch of coastal land separated each of the residences, providing a secluded, scenic experience for leisurely outings. But the arrival of a heavy rain had ruined any hope for a cliff-side stroll, and so the evening relegated itself to drinks and conversation.

Setting the needle down on a brand new vinyl record she'd purchased that morning, Lucia drowned out the sound of the rainfall battering the windows. Her husband, Renato, poured a glass of scotch into a tall, thin collins glass and escorted her down the steps into the sunken living room, where Henri and Carrol lounged atop the garishly colorful sofa.

Carrol had removed her heels, extending her bare feet out toward the suspended fireplace that hung down from the ceiling into the center of the circular living room. She curled and uncurled her toes, as though she were fanning the flames inside the hearth.

Lucia had always been jealous of Carrol's beauty. Raven hair and dark eyes. Somehow she'd maintained that exquisite body from her modeling years. A necessity, Lucia thought, in order to keep her well-off husband from losing interest. Though she knew the man's eyes were already wandering.

"Have you been up to the resort yet?" Henri asked, his free hand, the one not holding his scotch, rifling through the breast pocket of his saffron sport coat.

"Terme del Paradiso," Renato said, settling down on the velvet loveseat with Lucia. "It's a blemish on the beauty of Sicily."

Henri produced a pack of cigarettes from the pocket and lit one up.

Carrol took a sip from her glass. "I don't know. I think it looks rather attractive."

Henry expelled a puff of smoke into the air, where it hung above their heads. "It's all she's been able to talk about since we flew in. Been begging me to book us a room."

"Already tired of staying here with us?" Lucia asked.

"No, no, no." Carrol waved her off. "I meant after our weekend together. You both know there's nowhere else we'd rather be right now."

"For a minute there, I thought you were ready to break the tradition," Renato said.

Carrol pinched Henri's chin. "I would never dare think of such a thing. I know how badly you two men need your annual tête-à-tête."

"Yes, well, when you spend so much of your life with someone and he up and moves away to Rome, you have to cope somehow," Henri said, allowing Carrol's pinch to become a pull into a larkish kiss. As their lips parted, he turned to Renato and asked, "*Why* did you do that again?"

Renato faced Lucia and smiled. "I met someone special."

"Oh, yes. That's right. He fell in love."

Lucia imagined that Henri's ribbing hadn't evolved much since the two men were adolescents together. She'd often wondered what her husband would have been like had she known him in his youth. Henri had touted him to be quite the neighborhood ruffian, but Renato had refuted the picture his brother attempted to paint of his past, insisting he'd always been nothing but an absolute gentleman.

"That's right," Renato admitted. "I fell in love."

He clinked his glass against Lucia's and they both drank.

"You can relate to that, of course. Can't you, Henri?" Carrol gave him one of her looks. Lucia had seen it many times before. A brow raise and a smirk: a serious accusation wrapped in faux playfulness.

"Of course," Henri spouted. "Absolutely I can. We're lucky men, the two of us."

And they drank. All four of them.

Renato rose again, collecting the empty glasses to refill at the bar. He had poured the bottle of J&B into a crystal decanter before Henri and Carrol had arrived, a little touch he felt added to the prestige of the evening. He made a show of it, letting the scotch cascade down into each glass from the elegant container, then casually placed the crystal topper back into place. Stepping down into the conversation pit, he handed the ladies their drinks first.

Henri met Renato back at the bar and accepted the fresh beverage, then moved to the window wall, observing the rain pelting the glass. "Hell of a storm."

Renato strolled up beside him, shaking his head. "We always pick the best weekends, don't we?"

Lucia watched the two brothers as they stood shoulder to shoulder, looking out at the darkness.

"What do you think of it?" Carrol asked her.

Lucia turned, seeing Carrol pull her feet up onto the couch, tucking them in behind her like a schoolgirl ready for gossip.

"Sorry. What do I think of what?"

"The resort. Don't tell me you're against it as well."

"The resort. I haven't given it much thought, to be honest. I mean, it's been here for a few years now."

"But word has spread, as they say. It's not just some... what's the word I'm looking for?"

Lucia waited for Carrol to sort out her thoughts.

"Some... They're even talking about it in Vienna. That should tell you all you need to know." Carrol punctuated her sentence with an authoritative nod.

"I'm sure it's lovely," Lucia said. She looked over at her husband and Henri, both still gazing out at the rain.

"Do you ever worry about coming down here?" Carrol asked.

"How so?"

"You know. Because of the—" She leaned in closer, and mouthed the word *mafia*.

Lucia glanced behind her condescendingly, pretending as though she expected to see some villain in a suit ready to strike.

"Who are you afraid is going to hear you, Carrol?"

Carrol leaned back, surprised. Insulted even.

"It's not a humorous topic, Lucia. The influence that these people hold over Sicily is not—"

"Not worth discussing on our weekend retreat."

"I know people that have witnessed first-hand, mind you, the type of... of..." She shook her head, as though her words were too painful to allow residence in her mind, needing them to be thrown out.

Lucia extended a hand to settle her sister-in-law.

"Hey. I think most of that activity is in Palermo, anyway. Okay? No need to fret about it while we're here, safe in Taormina."

Carrol stared at Lucia's palm suspended in the open space between the two sofas. Nodding, she took a deep breath.

"Of course. You're right. Sometimes I just—" She massaged her temples and took another drink of scotch. "I feel a bit lightheaded."

Lucia struggled to hide her annoyance. Carrol was always one for the dramatics. Either she had a headache. Or she felt jet-lagged. Or a meal they shared didn't agree with her. Whatever ailment she could shoehorn into the situation to make herself the victim, Carrol would.

"You probably need to get something in your stomach. Let me get some fruit and—"

"Just something small," Carrol said. "I don't want you to go to any trouble."

"Of course," Lucia answered through her teeth.

As she passed Renato and Henri on her way out of the sunken living room, Renato asked, "Is everything all right?"

"Everything's great. Carrol's feeling lightheaded. Just needs something to eat. I'm going to see what I can put together."

"I can do it," Renato said, taking a step toward her.

"It's fine. I got it."

"I'll help then," Henri insisted. He motioned for Renato to accompany Carrol near the fireplace, then followed Lucia into the kitchen.

It was the first night of a long weekend, intended to start the vacation off with a lively tone, yet a few drinks in and Lucia had already found herself playing damage control. She pulled a bowl of berries from the refrigerator and put them under the faucet to wash.

"It *must* be good scotch," Henri said as he entered the kitchen. "I'm feeling lightheaded myself."

"Tolerance must be low, Henri. It's only a few J&B's."

He pressed himself up against her from behind, reaching around and grabbing one of the strawberries. He took a bite, but remained unnaturally close.

"What are you doing?"

"You know what I'm doing," he said.

It had been a year since the last time, and Lucia would have been lying to herself if she'd said she wasn't hoping he'd make another advance. But Renato and Carrol hadn't been in the house on that previous occasion. He'd taken her out duck hunting, leaving Lucia and Henri on their own, free to indulge *their* impulses without fear of being caught.

"Not now," she said, pushing him back with her hip.

She strained the berries and poured them from the colander onto a cloth to dry.

Henri pressed himself against her again, his hands grabbing her wrists, holding her in place between his body and the counter.

"What are you going to do? Fuck me right here in the kitchen?"

"Not a bad idea," he said.

"Don't be an idiot."

Henri's hand slid around her, his fingers slipping down between her stomach and skirt. "We'll be real quiet."

Lucia took a deep breath, closing her eyes.

"And if they walk in on us? Is that worth risking our marriages?"

His fingers traveled down between her legs.

"I'll admit, it would make the rest of the weekend rather awkward," he said.

"Now's not the—"

She bit her lip to keep from gasping as Henri's fingers entered her.

"I can't count on there being any duck hunting excursions to distract them this time," he said. "That is, if there even were one last year. Neither of them *did* come back with any dinner after all, *did* they?"

Henri kissed Lucia's neck as she looked over at the hallway leading to the living room. It looked blurry, and she felt her head begin to swim.

I guess it was *good scotch,* she thought.

With no further internal debate, her hand was reaching behind her, groping the front of Henri's pants. She could hear him smile, the wet edges of his mouth widening into a grin. Unzipping his pants, she slid her hand inside, grabbing hold of him, feeling him grow in her palm. She stroked once, but the restriction in the tight slacks was too inhibiting to continue.

As if sensing her frustration, he said, "Leave the water running," then guided her around the corner into the wood veneer paneled hallway beneath the open staircase.

He kissed her, his lips attempting to lock on, while hers pulled away, her head repeatedly leaning, checking to ensure they were alone.

"This is a bad idea," she breathed.

"We can be quick, yes?"

She listened intently for approaching footsteps, yet all she heard was the running sink, the rain assaulting the windows, and the smooth voice of Dean Martin crooning on the record player.

He guided her hand down.

She continued to watch for her husband and Carrol, as she began stroking him again. Her vision was becoming increasingly fuzzy, the details of the house distorting as though a thick fog had drifted in through an open window. Henri's hand settled on her shoulder and she felt him apply pressure to force her down.

"Not now," she said, still stroking.

"It'll make less of a mess this way. Don't want to ruin your skirt."

Her fingers clamped around his cock like a vise, her nails digging into the tender flesh. Henri winced in pain.

"I said, not now."

"Okay, okay." He tried to back away, but she held onto him to ensure her point had been made.

She kissed him once more and softly said, "We'll find a more opportune moment."

When she released him, he stumbled, tucking himself back into his pants for fear she may attempt to inflict more damage.

"Might want to calm yourself down a bit before you come out," she said, gesturing at the visible outline of his erection.

Walking back to the kitchen, she shut off the faucet and plated the berries, then strolled back out into the living room. Henri trailed behind, giving himself one final adjustment.

"Got something to help liven us up a bit," she said as she stepped down into the conversation pit, setting the plate of berries on the table between the two sofas.

Renato and Carrol were sitting beside one another, leaning in close. At first Lucia assumed they were whispering quietly to themselves, but upon further observation, she realized neither of them was talking. Neither of them were moving at all.

"Renato?"

As she took a step toward them, a nebulous cloud distorted her view — a misty film that seemed to slither across her eyes, obscuring her husband and Carrol as she approached.

Goddamn scotch. Why did Renato always insist on pouring so much?

"Carrol?" Henri said from behind her. The concern in his voice was unmistakable.

The two spouses remained motionless on the sofa.

Lucia crouched down in front of them to get eye level. "Don't tell me you passed—"

Lucia gasped.

Blood poured from a gaping wound across the front of Renato's neck. Something had savagely torn open the flesh, exposing bone and sinew. So too was Carrol's, ripped apart, displaying a grotesque aperture.

The ghastly sight sent Lucia falling onto her ass. She screamed, her heels and palms lurching her backward, sending her colliding into the floating fireplace. It jostled the metal, the hearth swaying, spilling embers out of the backside onto the tile floor. She turned, her knees and fingertips finding grip, raising her to her feet to escape the pit.

She grappled at Henri, who stood at the top of the steps, staring down in horror at the sight of his slain lover. Clawing up his legs, expecting the immediate embrace of consoling arms that never arrived, Lucia climbed to her feet, looking back over her shoulder at the expired bodies.

"Henri! Oh, God! Henri!"

The already distorted image of Renato and Carrol grew fuzzier. Lucia clung to Henri's frame, yet his arms remained limp at his side, as though he were so lost in the terrifying visage he hadn't even the strength to lift his hands.

Finally, Lucia looked up at him and saw the trickle of crimson snaking down over his bottom lip, dripping onto his lapel. It wasn't until the tip of the blade retracted from the center of his throat that she even noticed it was there. The movement. The way the light caught the metal, slick with blood.

Lucia screamed again. And the blade plunged into her abdomen. She felt it twist. Stumbling backward, the knife slid out of her as easily as it had entered. Her feet missed the steps, and she fell down into the sunken living room, crashing against the fireplace once again.

Settling on her back, her hand shot up in defense as Henri's body collapsed to a crumpled heap before her. The figure standing above was nothing but a murky shadow, blearing in and out of focus.

The scotch.

There was something in the scotch!

Rolling onto her side, Lucia's mind reeled.

Stop the bleeding. You need to stop the bleeding.

Her hands clamped around her stomach, fingers stuffing the loose material of her blouse into the wound.

"Help! Someone, please!"

The blade slashed down at her again, tearing open the fabric just below her breasts and grazing the flesh. She kicked up defensively, still screaming for help, then scooted away across the floor, sobbing, the image of her attacker morphing from the tears in her eyes and whatever villainous concoction had tainted the alcohol.

A gloved hand grabbed her by the hair, forcing her face against the fireplace. Shrieking in agony, Lucia could smell her skin sizzling as the killer held her against the black metal. One of her flailing legs found the killer's shin, and the gloved hand released her. Bubbling patches of her face lingered on the smoking hearth as she pulled free from the scalding fireplace.

Rising to her feet, she sprinted for the patio. With great effort, she slid open the heavy glass door and stumbled out onto the deck into the pouring rain, screaming for help with her remaining strength.

As she reached the railing, she looked back over her shoulder, seeing the killer following casually behind her. The patio light reflected in the blade as the figure raised the knife over its head, preparing to deliver the final blow. Without another thought, Lucia heaved herself over the railing just as the tip of the blade stabbed down into the lacquered wood.

For what seemed like ages, she fell, as if she were moving in slow-motion. When she finally hit the ground, she rolled through brush and bramble down a slope until she came to a halt at the edge of the cliff. The lights in the other beach houses had flared on, neighbors stepping out their front doors and peering through windows to see what all the commotion was about. Lucia knew there was nothing any of them could do to help her.

The water below was her only escape, but she wasn't sure she could clear the angular rocks at the base of the cliff. It wasn't that far of a drop, but the jagged stones could easily crack bone if she landed wrong. She mustered the strength to stand.

A tenebrous vignette was closing in around her eyes, her vision reducing to pinholes. The pouring rain. The rapid blood loss. The drugged scotch. She hoped the stab wound in her abdomen was still plugged with the gathered material from her shirt, but everything was so wet now, she couldn't be sure. When the knife had slid out of her, she felt the warm liquid cascading down her stomach, soaking the front of her skirt. But that warmth was gone now. All she could feel was the sting of the violent wind whipping raindrops against her ruined face.

Why was this happening to her? To her friends? Was it retribution for something? Some wrong they had committed against this stranger? Against the mafia, perhaps? She searched her fogging memory for answers that weren't there, just as a palm cupped her shoulder from behind and shoved her to her knees in the mud.

The elasticity of her skin popped easily as the blade pressed into her back. Somehow, she only felt one more stab. The rest of them only seemed to rock her aggressively as the hand tightened on her shoulder to hold her in place, like the harness of a rollercoaster steadying her as the ride jolted her about.

Thankfully, her sense of touch had fully gone now. It was all just... numb. But her other senses flared with extreme ability. Taste — iron in her mouth, drowning her tongue. Smell — sweet dewy mist blowing across the surface of the ocean. Sight — the glow of porch lights in the distance. And of course, sound — the morbid symphony of the long metal knife sliding in and out of her back, tearing her apart.

When the hand released, the weight of her limp torso pulled her to the ground, her face hitting the soil with a sort of disgusting squelch. There was no more reason to rationalize. No more reason to ask why.

It was simply time to let go.

Chapter 2
Jack Ivy & The Congressman

New Jersey.

Jack Ivy stood on the opposing side of the polished desk as Congressman Baylor flipped through the photographs in the manilla file, a permanent grin plastered across the politician's face.

"I was expecting favorable results, but these... these will guarantee a win, Jack." He looked up over his half-moon spectacles. "If they're real."

Jack stood confidently. "I'm a photographer, Congressman. Not a photo manipulator. What you see there is reality. Emulsion as fact."

Baylor held up one of the glossy prints and shook it with excited vigor. "This is Congressman Jennings, right here." He tapped his index finger against the photograph. "Mid-coitus with a whore."

"Whether the woman's a whore, I can't say," Jack replied.

"But it's not Jennings' wife."

Jack tilted his head, as if he'd not already examined the photos extensively. "I couldn't be quoted, sir. Nor would I be a reputable source."

"It's not his wife, Jack. I would know. This bitch is a fucking brunette, and Jennings' wife is a blonde. The public will see it for what it is."

Baylor set the photo down and picked up another, scanning it for all its details.

"Christ. And this one?" He laughed as though the photograph was some newly unearthed pile of treasure he'd prophetically discovered. "Is she fucking him from behind?"

"It was a rather creative encounter, Congressman," Jack said.

"My luck. This — hell, Jack. This is—"

"What you paid me for, sir."

The Congressman grinned. "That's right. That's goddamn right. You know, the police, they have power through force. The government gets power through agreements, handouts, perceived charity. But real power? Real power is photographic evidence, Jack. Truth. The dirty little secrets that scare the wealthy into succumbing to the threats of their enemies."

"It's none of my business how you use the photos, Congressman."

Baylor looked up at Jack with a condescending grin. "Right. Right. Because you're just the photographer. We're all criminals, son. It's just the sloppier you are, the easier you go down. And *you?*" He closed one eye, looking down his index finger at Jack as though it were the scope of a rifle. "You capture the sloppiness."

Jack nodded. "I'm glad to hear you're pleased with the results. Should I assume the payment has been—"

"Wired to your account? Of course."

He took a subtle step back from the desk, but before he could turn to leave...

"Wait just a moment, Jack."

The less time he had to spend in the Congressman's presence, the better. Jack knew Baylor's government paycheck wasn't the only way the man got paid. Rumors of La Cosa Nostra ties, people disappearing after disagreements, and other stories surrounded the Congressman, but no proof of crime had ever surfaced. Still, Jack knew Baylor was a dangerous man, and he was wise enough to know never to trust a politician to do anything other than what's in their own self-interest.

"As a bonus for your excellent work, I've arranged a little vacation for you," Baylor said.

Vacation? Just as Jack feared. He knew what that meant. Mafia slang for a long goodnight. He shouldn't have taken on the assignment. But, Christ, he needed the money. Rent had skyrocketed and good equipment wasn't cheap. If he didn't keep steady gigs, he'd be out on his ass before winter. Now he wasn't going to survive past 5pm.

"A vacation," Jack echoed, trying his best to not to alter his demeanor.

"A week in Sicily, at the resort my wife and I stayed at for our honeymoon. All expenses paid for."

Jack wasn't sure what to think. If Baylor was planning to knock him off now that the job was done, he didn't need to come up with an elaborate story about a trip to Sicily. Surely the man had associates who could put a bag over Jack's head and a belt around his throat as soon as he left the office.

"It's the most beautiful room in all of Taormina, Jack," Baylor said.

"I appreciate the offer, Congressman, but I'm not sure I—"

"Of course, you're worried you won't fit in, won't feel comfortable among the other guests who can afford such luxuries on their own. I can understand that. You're a man of the people. Fineries aren't something you normally allow yourself. But don't worry, my team will furnish you a full wardrobe so you can feel right at home at the resort."

Jack was hesitant, untrusting of the politician's offer, but he feared how things might escalate if he refused him. Again, the goons with the bag and belt were surely just beyond the office door if Baylor decided he needed them after all.

As if reading Jack's discomfort, Baylor said, "Listen, Jack. You've won me reelection with these photographs. After I put them to work, you're going to have a full-time gig. Do you understand that? Steady paychecks from here on out. You're about to become my personal surveillance detail, to monitor all of my... friends."

Jack bit his cheek. This wasn't a job offer. The Congressman had already decided for him. Jack had proven himself to be the master key to unlock any door for the Congressman with only a few shutter snaps of the camera.

"Congressman, I have other clients, people whose jobs I've already agreed to take on. I'm not sure I can drop all that and fly off to Italy."

Congressman Baylor chuckled. "Tell your other clients you're no longer open for business. You're no longer freelance."

Jack was in his pocket now, and he needed to find a way out. He couldn't concoct a sure-fire way off the cuff, so in an effort to buy himself some time, and avoid any immediate ramifications, he said, "Alright. I *have* heard Italy is beautiful. Thank you, Congressman."

"Good. Good. I want you to feel appreciated, Jack. And I want you to enjoy some relaxation before business gets booming. When you're back, we can talk details."

Jack tried to lean into optimism. How bad could it really be? A week long vacation before returning to a full-time job? Hell, how much more could he ask for? Regardless of how his political views aligned with Baylor's, money in the bank was money in the bank. And Jack was rarely one to let morality stand in the way of padding his pockets.

Chapter 3
Silvia Pasquale Checks In

Taormina, Sicily.

THE ATTENDANT OPENED the car door, revealing the front steps of the grand resort. Silvia Pasquale took the attendant's hand and stepped out, the wide brim of her hat and oversized sunglasses shielding most of her face from the Sicilian sun as she gazed up at the beauty of Terme del Paradiso. A pair of men in white suits with oversized lapels greeted her with requisite smiles.

"Welcome to Terme del Paradiso, Ms Pasquale," said the one with the meticulously groomed mustache.

"Grazie," she said, still absorbing the magnificence of the resort's exterior.

"We're very pleased to have you join us for your stay here in Sicily," he said. "I'm Aldo, the resort manager. This is Giancarlo, our concierge." Aldo gestured to the other man in the white suit.

Silvia nodded, smiling. The bellhop had already loaded her matching luggage from the trunk onto a cart beside them.

"Everything you require throughout your stay here at Terme del

Paradiso, my staff and I are here to see to. As you are aware, we are a five-star luxury resort, and the number one destination here in Sicily. Giancarlo would be happy to give you a tour on your way to your room."

"That would be lovely," Silvia said, watching as the bellhop pushed the luggage cart with her belongings past them to the access ramp.

"Don't worry about your bags, Ms Pasquale. They will be delivered to your room before your tour has ended."

"Of course," Silvia said, and followed Giancarlo through the front entry. The interior was no less impressive. More perfectly groomed staff members, waiting with permanent smiles, stood behind matching desks along a row of bone white pillars, which stretched to a vaulted ceiling decorated in gold reflective panels. It could have easily been mistaken for the scaly belly of some medieval dragon hovering above them.

"This is reception," Giancarlo said as Silvia removed her sunglasses. "We always have someone available here ready to assist with any questions you may have. You may call down to them from your room or visit in person if you prefer, and they will handle communication with all other departments at the resort. Room service. Spa reservations. Whatever you like."

They passed between two of the mighty pillars into the lobby where the dragon belly disappeared, replaced by a glass ceiling spilling sunlight down onto the handful of fashionable guests relaxing in an array of couches and armchairs while reading newspapers or sipping coffee. A pair of elevators on opposite sides rose and descended between the five floors, shepherding guests to their destinations.

"I like to call this the hub, because everything else spokes off from here. The pool to the west, the spa to the east, and the lounge and restaurant straight ahead to the south, each of them sure to be a high point of your stay."

Passing through the center of the lobby, Giancarlo led Silvia down an open hallway bordered with carved stone arches, keeping his pace casual as to give her ample opportunity to soak in every detail of the lavish architecture. "Naturally, we have a business center and conference rooms should you find a need to reserve one."

"I can't imagine I will," she said.

"The other amenities are far more enjoyable. No need to occupy oneself with work while on holiday, yes?" At the end of the hallway, he held open a door and let Silvia walk out first onto the terrace overlooking the grounds. "Beach access, fitness center, tennis courts, all of them available to you."

"It's beautiful," she said.

While Silvia's back was turned to him, Giancarlo looked her up-and-down. "Isn't it?"

She turned to face him, deciphering the slight change of tone in his voice. His eyes snapped back up to meet hers and he smiled widely.

"Shall I show you the spa next?"

"I think just my room would be fine for now."

Giancarlo gave a half bow and stepped aside to let Silvia back in through the doorway. The elevator ride to the fourth floor was silent, with Giancarlo smiling and nodding awkwardly each time he made eye contact with Silvia in the tight confines. His confidence was rattled after his exposed lingering gaze. Silvia pretended not to notice. She'd grown use to men ogling her, an everyday part of life since she was fourteen. Some would say men have no shame, but she knew that wasn't quite true. This man, Giancarlo, she could have scraped the shame off of him like a layer of burnt crannies from charred toast. But it wasn't shame for the ogling. It was the shame of being caught. It was the failure of his discretion, the embarrassment of allowing a witness. Situations like this never made men think to stop their leering, only to get better at hiding it.

Upon reaching room 411, Giancarlo unlocked and opened the door, handed Silvia the room key, repeated his spiel about "*should you need anything,*" then left her to her devices. She set her purse down on the end table and gave a quick inspection of her luggage, which had already been delivered, just as the resort manager had promised. Everything looked in order and she took a few moments to unpack and neatly arrange her outfits inside the hand carved wardrobe. With specificity, she placed every item from each suitcase somewhere in the room — the bathroom counter, vanity drawers, coat closet — until nothing remained inside any of the bags, which she then stacked in the far corner, out of sight behind the dinette set.

The bedroom window curtains had been pulled open prior to her arrival to show off the picturesque view of the beach. The waves gliding gently upon the shore, couples walking hand-in-hand, and a few yachts anchored in the bay. She took only a moment to observe, however, because while the sight was undeniably beautiful, she hadn't come all the way to Terme del Paradiso to stare at it from behind a pane of glass.

On her way back down to the main floor, the elevator stopped on each level, whereupon at each opening of the doors another guest or two entered, slowly filling the lift and forcing Silvia to the back. As with Giancarlo, the short ride was done in silence, and Silvia bid her time, staring at the backs of the guests in front of her until the doors opened a final time and everyone filed out.

Crossing through the lobby, she strolled into the lounge where a bartender and a barista worked in tangent behind the bar top, preparing late morning beverages for the handful of guests in sight. Silvia requested an espresso and while waiting for it to be made, she nonchalantly observed the other guests. There was a middle-aged couple who looked like old money, sitting in a pair of high back leather chairs, ignoring one another despite their proximity, as if their stay at the lavish resort were some sort of obligatory activity on their schedule. At the corner of the bar top, three young men, who Silvia found a bit rowdy for the current time of day, were laughing at one another's crude comments and quick, witty responses, all of them coated in a thick English accent.

And there was a man sitting on a sofa, dressed in black from head to toe, his eyes transfixed on Silvia with an expressionless, unblinking gaze. She nearly gasped, startled by his brazenness. Even after it was clear she had noticed him staring, the man refused to look away. He sat holding his coffee cup just below his chin, the steam slithering up in front of his gaunt face as he leered at her, gathering beneath the brim of his hat. The stylish accessory reminded Silvia of the old Dick Tracy comics she used to collect, but instead of a gangster-busting detective donning it, the hat perched atop the head of a villainous-looking man in a black raincoat.

"Your espresso, ma'am," said the barista, breaking the tense stare down and stealing Silvia's attention.

"Grazie," she said, taking it from the counter. When she looked back, the man in black had set his drink down on the table beside him, and was reading from a paperback novel, his interest in Silvia extinguished.

"This is your first time at Terme del Paradiso?" the barista asked.

"Yes. I'm familiar with the area, but it's my first time staying at the resort," said Silvia.

"The terrace just out those doors has one of the best views in all of Sicily. There's no better place to enjoy an espresso." Silvia looked to where the barista was gesturing, smiled, thanked her, and took her suggestion.

The panoramic view of the coast was exactly what Silvia wanted: white sand beaches intertwined with stunning cliffs, and transparent water stretching out endlessly. The beauty of it was so striking that she hadn't immediately noticed there was someone else on the terrace with her.

A man, dressed in expensive-looking casual attire, was leaning on the railing with his cup of coffee, staring out at the bay. Sensing her presence, he glanced at her over his shoulder then straightened up and raised his cup in a *cheers* fashion. "Morning," he said with a charming smile. Silvia could tell from his accent he was American.

"Good morning," Silvia replied.

Surprisingly, the American turned back to the bay, leaving the choice of continuing the conversation solely on Silvia. She paused a moment, drank the entirety of her espresso, then approached the railing several feet away. Facing the beach, she watched from her peripherals, waiting for him to glance over at her again. When he did, she expected him to start with the usual pleasantries, but he just smiled again and turned back to the view.

"You're American?" The words came out almost instinctually. She wasn't used to being the one to initiate conversations with strange men, and the words felt awkward as she heard them escape her mouth.

He turned to her once again. "I am. Arrived just yesterday."

"What brings you to Terme del Paradiso?" She wasn't sure why she was suddenly forcing herself to engage with the man. Sure, he was handsome, but she crossed paths with handsome men daily. No, it had to be his indifference to her — his casualness. It intrigued her. She suddenly felt angry with herself for letting what was almost certainly this man's way of luring in women get the better of her, and considered walking away right then.

"Oh, just a little vacation. You?"

"I'm... here to meet someone — meet *with* someone."

"You sound Italian."

"Sì," she said. "Good guess."

He laughed, raised his cup again in the same *cheers* fashion and took another drink. "I ought to win an award for my detective skills, right?"

"Very impressive," she said with a grin.

"My name's Jack. Jack Ivy."

"Silvia Pasquale."

"Pleasure to meet you, Silvia Pasquale."

"And you, Jack."

They both laughed quietly, amused by the banter.

"How long are you here for?" he asked.

"Seven days. I arrived just now."

"Wonderful. I look forward to seeing you around then."

"I'll be around."

Jack finished what was left of his coffee and said, "Ciao, Silvia."

"Ciao, Jack Ivy."

And he strolled away, back inside the resort.

The brief but pleasant interaction had almost made Silvia forget all about the unnerving man in black. Through the windows she could see him in the lounge, still sitting alone reading his book. Something about him seemed familiar, but she couldn't quite place it.

Chapter 4
The Filmmaker

Jack tried to push aside the looming angst of his inevitable career path and enjoy the amenities of the resort while he had the means to do so. He filled the rest of his day with a trip to the spa, where he enjoyed a massage (the first he'd ever had), then a nap in his room, followed by a shower and shave. He picked out a leisure suit from the wardrobe the Congressman's people had fashioned for him and readied himself for a trip down to the lounge for some dinner and drinks.

Jack couldn't help but imagine this is what a casual cocktail party would be like in a multi-millionaire's living room. Mood lighting, comfortable seating, and a pianist in jacket and tie providing soft ambient tunes. The room was divided into two areas; the bar and cocktail seating on one side, and the dining area on the other, though the two flowed seamlessly together, separated only by a few decorative pillars. Harvest gold paint accented the marble surfaces. An illuminated back bar with symmetrical arches, displaying every brand of liquor one could call for, was the focal point.

"Americano, please," Jack said as he slid onto one of the swiveling barstools. He watched as the bartender filled an old-fashioned glass with ice, then poured in equal parts Campari and sweet vermouth before topping with soda water and garnishing with an orange slice. The bartender placed the cocktail atop a marble coaster in front of Jack, then extended his hand across the bar to shake hands.

"My name's Luca," he said.

Jack shook his hand. "Jack." Then he tasted the beverage and nodded approvingly. "Absolutely perfect."

"Thank you, sir," he nodded courteously. "Glad you like it."

"I didn't see you here yesterday, Luca."

"No, I'm off on Thursdays. I'm usually the mid-bartender Friday through Tuesday."

"Mid-bartender?"

"Middle shift bartender. My shift overlaps with the morning and late night teams. I get the luxury of not having to be here bright and early, and also don't have to be the last one out. The perks of seniority."

"Sounds like a good gig," Jack said.

"You won't ever hear me complain about it."

As Luca walked to the other end of the bar to attend to another customer, Jack observed the other guests in the lounge. He felt like a fraud sitting there among the wealthy and privileged. Back in the States when he'd be on a job, trailing some unfaithful high-profile somebody who'd stopped into a swanky nightclub, he could never afford to order a cocktail like this. He always stuck to water, asking the bartender to pour it into a rocks glass so as not to stick out more than he already did. Somehow, even with all the glamour, fineries and amazing views, the guests of Terme del Paradiso all seemed a bit bored, as though their life of luxury, which many would have killed for, was a kind of burden. Jack couldn't reconcile it.

"You a fan?" Luca asked as he approached again.

"Excuse me?"

"Of Elio's." Luca could see by the look on Jack's face that he had no idea what he was referring to. "Elio Gaeta. The man in all black over there. You were looking at him."

Jack glanced in the direction that Luca nodded, seeing the man he was referencing sitting at a table just inside the dining room.

"I was sort of looking at everyone, guess."

"You don't know of him?" Luca asked.

"Should I?"

"He's a famous Italian filmmaker. *Vita Erotica? Wet Walls & Big Bounties? Bitches Bleed Red?* No?"

"Sorry. I don't watch many Italian pictures."

Jack looked over at Elio again, this time noticing the radiant young woman sitting at the table with him.

"Who's she?"

"Vittoria Gaeta. His wife. A model, of course. What else for the great Elio Gaeta?" The snark in Luca's voice was unmistakable.

Jack took a drink of his cocktail and continued to watch the supposedly famous couple. A waitress stopped at their table to check on the meal, and Jack saw Elio's hand stroke the woman's hip with blatant vulgarity. Shocked, the waitress immediately stepped back, and Vittoria scolded her husband. Elio laughed and when Vittoria chided him again, the filmmaker's demeanor darkened and he pulled back his hand over the opposite shoulder, as if preparing to strike his wife across the face. Then he softened, mumbled something at her in Italian, and went back to eating his dinner. Vittoria sat stoically, either too upset or too shook to touch her food.

"Quite the individual," Jack said to Luca.

"Yes, quite," Luca agreed.

"*Bitches Bleed Red*, you said?"

"One of those erotic lesbian vampire films. He's a horror filmmaker, mostly. *Wet Walls & Big Bounties* was his stab at making a western, just a bunch of soldiers slaughtering American Indians. You can dress it up in a cowboy hat, but horror is still horror."

Elio looked up from his plate with a mouthful of pasta and locked eyes with Jack. He rolled his eyes and leaned back in his chair, grumbling something as though the great filmmaker had just been discovered by unwanted paparazzi. He looked away, shielding the side of his face with his palm, and then glanced back to see if Jack was still staring. Jack chuckled, amused by the dramatic overreaction.

"What do you suppose would frustrate him more?" Jack asked Luca. "If I went over to speak with him? Or if I didn't bother to look over there again at all?"

Before Luca could answer, Jack was out of his stool and walking over to Elio's table, cocktail in-hand. He could see Elio mutter something to Vittoria, who looked over her shoulder, seeing Jack for the first time.

"Excuse me," Jack said, stopping beside the table. "I'm Jack." Vittoria looked him up and down, immediately intrigued, but as soon as Jack said he was a fan of her husband's and wanted to buy him a drink, she rolled her eyes and went back to her glass of wine.

Elio feigned annoyance for a moment, then said, "Well, you clearly have wonderful taste in films. Of course, join us."

"Gratzi," Jack said. Vittoria smirked at his poor Italian accent. Jack motioned to the waitress, ordered Elio another cocktail and instructed for it to be put on his tab at the bar.

"Are you here shooting a film?"

"We're enjoying a brief hiatus before I jump into my next project," Elio answered.

"How exciting! May I ask what it is?"

"Oh, now... I can't really discuss it."

"Oh. Of course."

The three of them sat in awkward silence until the waitress returned with a Negroni for Elio. When the filmmaker noticed Jack soaking in Vittoria's beauty, he gave in. "Alright, I guess I can share a bit. But it doesn't leave this table."

Jack gave him his full attention.

"It's called *No Mask For Breathing*. It's about a famous scuba diver who murders his wife after she's unfaithful to him."

"Sounds suspenseful."

"It may end up being my best work."

"That'd be something."

Elio nodded and drank. "So, what's your favorite? Of my films, I mean."

"Well," Jack chuckled. "That's a tough question."

"So many good ones." Vittoria's words were drenched in sarcasm.

Elio's jaw clenched, but he thought better of raising his voice again.

"*Black Sunday!*" Jack said, slapping his hand on the tabletop. "Now that was one hell of a film."

"*Black Sunday?*" Elio furrowed his brow. "*Black Sunday?*"

"It was great. Don't be modest about it. I really liked *Marnie* too."

A grin crossed Vittoria's face as she realized Jack's true motive for sitting down. With each film he listed that Elio had no part in creating, her interest in Jack intensified.

"You're confused," Elio said. "Mario Bava did—"

But Jack cut him off. "I didn't really enjoy *Wet Walls & Big Bounties*, though. But you can't expect them all to be masterpieces." Jack pretended not to notice the growing fury on Elio's face. "I hope that doesn't offend you. Your other films, I loved them all."

"Did you?"

Jack stood and adjusted his suit jacket. "I appreciate you taking the time to speak with a fan. I'll leave the two of you to your dinner," he said, and strolled back over to the bar top, where Luca stood, unable to hide the smile on his face.

To Jack's surprise, the woman, whom he'd met earlier that morning on the terrace, was perched on a bar stool, her fingers grazing the stem of a fresh martini.

"Hey!" Jack pointed at her instinctively. "Uh, Silvia, right?"

"Jack Ivy," she said with a coy grin.

Jack sat down beside her.

"Friend of yours?" She gestured at Elio.

"Him? No. Just met him. Giving him a good ribbing is all. Luca here tells me he's a rather notable filmmaker."

Silvia gave Elio another glance. "Of course. I knew he looked familiar. Elio Gaeta."

"That's him," Jack said.

"So you came all this way to mock Italian filmmakers?"

"I don't know if *mock* is the right word," he said. She raised an eyebrow. "Okay. Yeah, you're right. Mock is the *perfect* word."

Silvia laughed through her nose.

"You're a fan?" Jack asked her.

"Of Elio Gaeta's? Hardly. You should have seen how he was looking at me this morning, just before I met you, actually. The man is an absolute creep. I feel bad for his wife."

Jack glanced back at Elio's table and caught Vittoria looking over her shoulder in his direction. When he smiled, she grinned back, then turned away to face her oblivious husband.

"Yes," Jack said. "Poor woman." Then he straightened up and gave Silvia his undivided attention. "Look, if you're planning on having another drink after the one you're enjoying, I'd be happy to buy it for you."

"If I decide to have another, you'll be the first to know. I'm not much of a drinker."

"Neither am I," Jack admitted. "Alcohol rarely agrees with me. Caffeine, on the other hand, I can drink it from sunrise to sunset."

"It doesn't keep you up at night?"

"Oh, I'm sure it contributes, but I enjoy being up late. The calm of late nights and early mornings when everyone else is asleep can be quite relaxing."

"I'm certain any time of day at this resort is relaxing."

"You said you were here to meet with someone?" Jack asked. He could see the discomfort wash over her.

"That's right."

"I apologize," Jack said quickly. "We don't need to discuss it. I'm just making conversation."

"No, it's fine. Really. I'm here in Sicily to reunite with my father. I haven't seen him in many years."

Jack nodded. "I'm no stranger to having an estranged family."

The crash of a wine glass shattering across the floor made them both jump. They spun around to see Elio standing at his table, pointing his index finger at Vittoria, his face cherry red, the veins in his forehead throbbing with such pressure they looked like serpents beneath the skin. He shouted at her in Italian, brandishing his finger like a knife at her chest. The restaurant manager hurried over, attempting to deescalate the situation. He whispered, trying to calm Elio, who eventually sat back down in his chair, slapping the tabletop and jangling the china plates and silverware as a final act of defiance. Then the manager thanked him and left them to resume whatever conversation had sparked the heated exchange.

"Jesus," Jack said.

Silvia shook her head and sipped her drink. "Bastard."

Jack turned to Luca, who was mixing up a martini, and asked, "Aren't they going to do anything about him?"

"I'm sure the manager will have him leave if it happens again. A warning is customary. You'd be surprised how often people get a bit out of hand here."

"If you're rich, you can get away with almost anything," Silvia said.

One of the resort attendants motioned for Luca at the other end of the bar, and Luca went to him. Jack saw the attendant point his way, then Luca nodded, strolled back over to Jack and Silvia and said, "Call for you at reception, Jack."

"For me?"

"That's what they told me."

Silvia slugged back the rest of her cocktail and set the empty glass on the bar. "It's time I retire, anyway."

"I'm sure it will only take a moment," Jack said to her. "Stay, please. I'd love to buy you that second drink."

"I never agreed to have a second," she said. "I'll see you tomorrow if you're around."

"Alright then." Jack stood. "I'll be around."

He made his way through the lounge, to the front reception area, giving one last glance at Silvia before he turned the corner out of sight.

"Call for Jack Ivy?" Jack said to the concierge.

The man gestured like a magician toward the receiver resting on the desk. Jack scooped it up and held it to his ear.

"This is Jack."

"Jack," the Congressman's voice purred on the other end of the line. "How's Sicily treating you?"

"Just perfectly, Congressman."

"Everything I told you it would be, right?"

"Everything and more." Even if it hadn't been, Jack was smarter than to express anything but gratitude to his new employer.

"I called your room first. Silly me to think you wouldn't be down at the bar at this hour. Easy to forget about the time difference."

"Of course. And how are things back home?"

"Oh, don't you worry about any of that right now. Plenty of time to dive into the nitty gritty when you get back. I just wanted to check in and be sure you're enjoying yourself."

"I couldn't ask for a grander vacation, sir."

"Good, good. Listen, when you tire of that gorgeous restaurant there at the resort, there's a nice little eatery down the road, a purple building with a yellow roof, little bistro tables out front. It's worth a visit."

"I'll do that."

"Take care of yourself, Jack. Don't get into too much trouble."

Jack heard the click of the call disconnecting. He handed the receiver to the concierge and thanked him before heading back to the lounge.

As he turned the corner, he could see that Silvia's chair was now vacant. He cursed under his breath, the brief glimmer of hope that she might still be there waiting for him, quickly evaporating. No bother. He'd see her again tomorrow. He had run into her twice in one day, after all. Maybe he'd even be able to convince her to go with him to that eatery Congressman Baylor had mentioned.

Taking a seat at the bar again, he saw Luca removing his apron and gathering his belongings. "You're leaving too?"

"Headed home. Shift is over," Luca said. He patted the other bartender on the shoulder. "This is Andrea. He's a fantastic bartender.

Not as good as me, but still plenty skilled to handle your drinks for the rest of the evening."

"It was a pleasure talking with you," Jack said.

Luca folded his apron and slid it into his bag. "Likewise. And I appreciate the entertainment you provided. We can talk films again tomorrow if you stop in."

"I'll do that."

"And I'll remember your drink."

Luca tipped an invisible hat, strolled out from behind the bar and disappeared around the corner toward the front doors of the resort.

"Another drink for you, sir?" Andrea asked.

Jack shifted the lonely ice around in his glass as he debated. The grumbling voice of Elio Gaeta snared his attention, and he glanced over to see Vittoria helping her visibly drunk husband through the lounge. She braced him with one arm behind his back, her hand hooked around under the opposite armpit, and the other gripping his elbow to help him balance. He muttered to himself, and even though the words had been in Italian, Jack could tell they were severely slurred. As they passed by, Vittoria made eye contact with Jack, and the slightest grin curved into existence. A matching eyebrow raised, and she kept her sights locked on him all the way to the elevator. It wasn't until the doors closed, sealing the couple inside, that the gaze finally broke.

Jack slid his glass toward the new bartender. "Yes. I'll have one more."

Chapter 5
The Terrified Little Girl

Vittoria Gaeta, who until two years prior had been Vittoria Rossini, grew up in post-war Rome with her widowed mother. A clothing designer by trade, her mother stepped back into the workforce as soon as she was able, immersing Vittoria in the world of high fashion. Vittoria spent countless days sitting in the corner of her mother's shop watching her sew the most beautiful gowns. By night she attended runway shows, watching in silence from the rafters while her mother sat with the other invitees below. Her fascination with the modeling world burgeoned, and at fourteen she donned one of her mother's gowns for her first catwalk. It was a high-speed ride from that point on, her confidence and beauty snaring the attention of several big industry names.

Her modeling career grew feverish over the next eight years, with nearly every prominent designer in Rome seeking her out, and just as her fame looked as if it were about to peak, she was invited to audition for a role in her very first film. Seeing it as an opportunity to gain perhaps an even greater level of fame, Vittoria jumped at the chance. Her manager briefed her during their car ride over to the Grand Hotel, citing the notable filmography of the director she was about to meet.

She took the elevator up to the fourteenth floor as her manager had instructed and when she rapped on the door to room 1411, she felt her nerves crescendo into an opera of anxiety. She hadn't felt that type of unease since her first catwalk all those years ago. Each subsequent event had seemed to get easier than the last, yet standing there in the hotel hallway, she felt so very nervous.

The door opened and a young woman, who Vittoria guessed was only a few years older than her, offered a greeting and ushered her inside the suite. All the furniture had been shoved against the walls, opening up the floor space for where Vittoria assumed the audition would take place.

"Wait here, please," the woman said before hurrying off through the double doors of the bedroom. Vittoria could hear her whispering to someone, but couldn't quite make out what was being said. Then the woman emerged once more, touched Vittoria gently on the arm and bid her, "Good luck," before leaving the hotel room altogether.

In the modeling world, it wasn't uncommon for her to audition alone for a designer. But usually those auditions took place in studios, empty conference rooms, and occasionally a warehouse repurposed for event hosting. Never a hotel room. But this was the film world, and she figured that in the film world, things were done a bit differently. Maybe this was the norm. She hoped that was the case. She hoped she hadn't been left alone for some ulterior purpose, helpless against whatever was about to unfold.

And suddenly that was all she could imagine.

What had she walked into?

She thought about leaving. She could still run out the door, take the elevator down and get back outside into the sunshine. Into the highly populated city with plenty of witnesses. But her manager would throw a fit. She'd worked hard to arrange the details for the audition, setting up accommodations, having a new outfit specially made. She'd be furious if Vittoria ruined it all because she got frightened. And frightened of what, exactly? Some made-up scenario in her head? No. She couldn't rationalize that. She couldn't explain to anyone, much less her manager, why she ran out of the hotel like a scared schoolgirl.

She tried to steady her nerves, shoving the foreboding feeling into the back of her mind. Then a voice from the bedroom cut through the collage of thoughts swirling about her head.

"I'm a big fan of yours."

Vittoria kept her feet planted but leaned a bit, trying to see into the bedroom. "Pardon?"

"I said, I'm a fan." The man's voice was kind, warming the goosebumps on Vittoria's arms into nonexistence.

"Oh. Thank you."

Elio Gaeta strolled out of the bedroom, buttoning the sleeves of his black shirt. He took a seat on the couch that had been shoved against the wall Vittoria was facing, and said, "Sorry about the mess. I asked them to remove the furniture completely, so we'd have more room, but they said they didn't have anywhere else to store it."

"It's fine," Vittoria responded, catching herself standing too casually and quickly straightened up into a tighter pose.

"I love that dress," he said, gesturing with a lazy hand.

"Thank you. The designer did a wonderful job."

"As impressive as a gown may look, it always looks better on a beautiful body."

Vittoria forced a smile. She was used to getting compliments like that during auditions. Although still somewhat crude, she always preferred them over the kind she would hear while walking down the street.

"I've seen you on the runway many times," he said. "I attend a good many fashion shows, you know?"

"I'm surprised I haven't noticed you."

"Well, you are, of course, so focused on your walk, making it look perfect. I like to sink into the shadows a bit myself. The less attention I get in public, the better."

"You're a famous film director. It must be hard not to draw attention."

"I prefer my films do the talking for me. I want everyone's eyes glued to the celluloid, not the man behind the curtain. But *you* like attention, right? You like knowing people's eyes are lingering on you."

Vittoria's goosebumps resurfaced. "I don't know if I'd put it quite that way."

"No? That's a shame, because I'm looking for someone who craves just that. I'm looking for someone who wants to be a star, one that shines so brightly men can't help but stare."

"I've never acted before."

"That's a lie. You're acting right now. You're pretending to be comfortable with this interaction, while inside you're questioning yourself for even entertaining this meeting. And so far you're doing a hell of a job at it." Elio crossed one leg over the other and leaned back into the couch. "Shall we see how far you can take this character? Push your limits? Because that's what this audition is all about. I need to see if you can play the role, become the character, leave the terrified little girl locked deep inside, and wear the mask of a confident femme fatale."

Terrified little girl?

Vittoria's jaw clenched. She wasn't about to let this smug man intimidate her any further. If he wanted to see a performance, she'd give him one. She knew whether or not she got the role, she could at least tell her manager that she'd given it her all. She could walk out knowing she hadn't surrendered to her fear. Christ, she did her first catwalk at fourteen. Even then, she was brave and confident. Even then, she was pushing her limits. She knew she was *still* that same person.

"Aren't you supposed to give me a script or something to read?" Vittoria asked bluntly.

Elio smiled.

Six months later, they had wrapped filming on *Bitches Bleed Red*. Vittoria had played the role of a call girl who gets murdered in an alleyway after nearly exposing the film's villain. During the grueling shoot, Vittoria became enraptured by Elio and his passion for the project. She had never met anyone as fully dedicated to his craft. It impressed her, excited her, and on the night of the wrap party, when Elio attempted to seduce her, she countered with her own aggressive advance, resulting in a booze-soaked fuck in the wine closet of the restaurant. One of the staff members walked in on them and by the next week, tabloids were printing about the alleged affair between the brooding filmmaker and the model-turned-actress-turned-muse.

The press fueled the fire of their blossoming romance, fanning the flames of excitement to a fever pitch that culminated in Elio proposing to Vittoria three months after they began dating. The two wed in Rome a year later, then dove into preparation for Elio's next film project, *Cold Grave For A Hot Harlot.*

That's when things changed for Vittoria. The infatuation stage ended, and life as Elio's wife morphed from glitzy parties with celebrities and luxurious vacations with wealthy friends, to long evenings alone and drunken arguments stemming from Elio's growing promiscuity.

It was just before the filming of *Cold Grave* was about to begin that Elio gave the role he had written for Vittoria to another actress – some eighteen-year-old who'd never done a film in her life. Elio said that the film needed a fresh face, someone the world had never seen before. He said everyone knew who Vittoria Gaeta was, and that it would be easier for the audience to buy into the character if he cast an unknown.

Vittoria was crushed. She'd spent months preparing for the role, learning the script forward and backward, discussing character motivations and backstories with her husband ad nauseam. And for what? To be replaced last minute by some little bitch? But when she argued the point, Elio quickly shut her down, saying he wouldn't let anyone infringe on his artistic vision, that he and he alone knew what was best. He offered Vittoria a smaller role to appease her, but she refused, stating she'd never again be involved in any of his films. Not after such a betrayal.

And that was when Elio Gaeta first began writing the outline for a future project, one about a famous scuba diver who murders his wife after she cheats on him. He shared the details of his progress on the new script with Vittoria over countless silent dinners. She listened to him go on an on about the character of the wife who deserted her husband emotionally, how the woman had pretended to be his partner but in truth had been a villainous siren all along. It was a clumsy attempt at a metaphor, she thought. The great Elio Gaeta was slipping. Past his prime. The man had become a shadow of his once great self — or perhaps he had never been all that great to begin with. Perhaps Vittoria had just been swept up in the excitement. Yes, that was it. She'd allowed herself to be fooled. Allowed herself to ignore the warning signs and dive headfirst into the shallow pool that was Elio Gaeta.

But it wasn't too late to get out. She could still abandon his washed-up ass and get a fresh start. She could go back to modeling, or maybe she could audition for some other films, ones not headed by an egotistical creep. It wouldn't even be that hard, either. The only thing left to decide was when to do it — the ideal time to tell Elio she was leaving him.

When he told her they'd be traveling to Sicily so he could decom-press before jumping into pre-production of the new film, she knew it would be the perfect opportunity to do it. She'd wait until their final night there, so that the news would still be fresh in his mind, maybe even enough to distract him while on set. Maybe he wouldn't be saddened by the notion of divorce, but Vittoria knew he'd most assuredly be enraged by it. He'd see it as an insult, a blemish on his image. Famous filmmaker divorced by model wife. The article headlines would soak up all the attention from the news of a new Gaeta film being shot.

It would be her revenge. Elio Gaeta would rue the day that he had ever invited that terrified little girl to audition for one of his films.

Vittoria leaned the drunken mess that was Elio Gaeta against the inner wall of the elevator as it rose to the third floor of Terme del Paradiso. He steadied his swaying body against the handrail, closing his eyes and mumbling to himself. Vittoria stared at him, the half untucked shirt beneath his wrinkly black suit jacket, the scuffed dress shoes, and the red stain of Campari on his lips. How different he looked after the few short years she'd known him. But she knew this was the true Elio, not that eerily charming man she had met in the hotel three years earlier. It wasn't only Vittoria who had put on a performance that day. Elio turned out to be quite the actor himself. But now the charade was over, the mask removed, and she was left with the ghoulish truth.

The elevator doors opened and Vittoria helped him down the hall to their room, where she shoved him down across the bed. His eyes remained closed, drool draining from his crooked jaw, and he began to snore. Vittoria thought about removing his shoes or jacket, but quickly thought better of displaying such kindness. She poked at his gut a few times to see if he'd wake, then slapped him lightly across his bloated cheek, neither attempt rendering a response.

"Elio," she whispered. He snored louder. *"Elio!"* He twitched and farted and rolled onto his side, still hard asleep. Confident he was out for the night, Vittoria went to the mirror, checked her makeup, then strolled out the door, leaving Elio alone in the darkness.

Returning to the lounge, she was pleased to see that the American who had done such a fine job of insulting her husband was still sitting at the bar. She sat down on the stool beside him, reveling in the surprise on his face.

"Back for another?" he asked.

"The night is still young."

"In that case, let me buy you a drink." The American flagged down the bartender and said, "Whatever the lady is having, put it on my tab."

"Actually," Vittoria spoke up. "I'd like you to charge my drink, as well as everything this gentleman here has rung up, to my room."

The bartender nodded.

"Your husband won't mind?" the American asked.

"Oh, I'm sure he'll mind plenty. But I'm doing it, anyway." She looked at the bartender and said, "What do you recommend?"

"The gentleman is drinking an Americano. Campari, sweet vermouth, sparkling water. An excellent drink," the bartender said.

"Sounds perfect." She turned back to the American as the bartender began mixing up the cocktail. "What did you say your name was?"

"Jack."

"Jack." She didn't hide the fact that she was sizing him up.

"Go ahead. Ask what you're wanting to ask," Jack said.

"You had no idea who my husband was before tonight, did you?"

"No, I did not."

"He has his share of agitators, and their passionate disdain seems to fuel him just as much as the people who love him. But there is one thing that truly upsets him, truly offends him, and that's people who don't know or care about him."

"Well, I'm sorry if I offended him."

"No, you aren't."

Jack grinned. "No, I'm not."

The bartender set the fresh Americano down in front of Vittoria. "Grazie." She took a sip, and both men waited for her reaction. "Perfetto."

They both smiled, and the bartender moved on to another guest.

"So it was intentional, then?" Vittoria asked. "To offend him?"

"A means to an end."

"And what exactly *was* that end?"

"To get your attention. As much as your husband seems to want the eyes of the world, I simply want yours."

"Is that so?"

"It is."

"Well, Mr. Jack... you have them." She raised her glass to cheers. Their glasses clinked together, and they locked eyes as they drank. "What is it you do when you're not trying to lure women away from their husbands?"

Jack laughed. "I guess, uh, I'm a bit of a photographer."

"A model and a photographer walk into a bar — sounds like the setup to a bad joke."

"Can't wait for the punchline."

"Are you here on business, then?"

"Not at all. Strictly vacation."

"Thought you might be in town to photograph some Italian models. Lot of beautiful women in Sicily."

"Unfortunately, nothing that exciting," Jack admitted.

"That's a shame. Maybe someday you and I will end up doing a photoshoot together."

"Just so happens I've got my camera up in my room."

Vittoria laughed. "You *are* bold, aren't you? First you insult my husband to his face, then you invite me to model for you in your hotel room?"

"What's your husband doing at the moment?" Jack asked.

"Drooling into his pillow."

"Aren't you afraid he'll wake up?"

"He'll be out for hours."

She sipped her drink. He sipped his.

Moments later, the elevator doors spread open as Vittoria and Jack stumbled inside in the midst of a passionate embrace. Jack kissed her neck, his hands traversing along the seam of her dress. Her hand slid down the front of his pants, grabbing him, feeling him grow in her palm. She realized too late that the doors had opened again and turned to see one of the resort maids standing a few feet away. The woman's eyes were wide with shock at the sight of the lurid display. Vittoria released Jack and composed herself.

"Excuse us," Jack said to the maid, then took Vittoria by the hand and led her briskly down the hallway to his room. The maid watched them with a craned neck as Jack unlocked the door and pulled Vittoria inside.

He kicked the door closed as Vittoria undid his tie. His hands struggled with the tiny zipper on the back of her dress, and wasting no time, she reached around herself to take control.

"Get your pants off," she said.

Jack did as he was told, removing his shoes in the process.

Her dress hit the floor, and she stepped out of it, grabbing hold of Jack's shirt and quickly undoing each button. They kissed, locking onto one another as their hands continued to strip off the remnants of clothing. Vittoria shoved Jack backward onto the bed, then straddled him briefly before he grabbed her ass and lifted her up and onto her back. He rolled over on top of her, kissing her again.

It had been years since she'd felt like this. Years since someone had embraced her with such passion. The excitement of being in this stranger's bed, his tongue on her skin, it was almost unbearable.

Their eye contact did not break as she watched him wet his fingers and enter her. Then her neck went slack and her back arched, her legs spreading wider. She let him tease her for a few minutes, feeling his fingers dancing to some inaudible tune, then she grabbed him by the wrist.

He stopped, his eyes returning to hers.

"Fuck me," she said.

He hovered over her and when she felt him graze against her, she wrapped her legs around his waist, pulling him in tight, forcing him inside. Her hands slid down his chest, feeling the muscles flexing. She moaned as he leaned back and grabbed her by the waist, lifting her ass off the sheets as he continued to thrust. His index and middle finger slid into her open mouth, gently pulling on her lower jaw. She sucked as he continued to fuck her. Harder. Faster.

It had only been like this once with Elio, back in that wine closet at the wrap party. He'd fucked her like she was the most desirable woman he'd ever encountered. He fucked her as if it were the last time he'd ever be able to touch a woman. The ultimate finale. Elio made her feel like a star that night, and there in the American's hotel room, she once again felt like the belle of the ball.

When the two of them eventually became too exhausted to move, they laid beside one another, unashamed in their nakedness atop the sheets, staring out the window at the moonlit waves. Jack reached across and pulled her in close.

"I still have that camera if you're up for it," he quipped.

Vittoria laughed and nestled in closer. "Maybe next time."

They laid together awhile longer, then Vittoria slapped his leg gently and got out of bed to collect her things.

"Leaving?"

"Elio won't be asleep forever," she said as she pulled her underwear up.

"Don't want him getting suspicious."

She smiled, and zipping up her dress, said, "This was nice, Jack. I'm glad you were still there when I returned."

"And I'm glad you returned."

She leaned over the bed to kiss him goodbye and he pulled her in on top of him, kissing her wildly all over. She laughed, pushing him away, playfully struggling to break free of his grip.

"Don't! No, stop! I'm serious now. I need to go!"

"Okay, okay." He said, releasing her from the bed.

She opened the door a crack, peering out to check for any witnesses, then turned back to Jack in bed and said, "Till next time."

"I'll have the camera ready."

She grinned, slid through the door, and closed it gently behind her. Making her way down the hall, she had to stop and brace herself against the wall to adjust the strap on her shoe. She caught her reflection in the golden glow of the elevator doors and shook her head at the sight of herself.

A bit rough looking, aren't you, love?

She brushed her hair back behind her ears, trying to smooth out the rogue strands, then rubbed at the smeared lipstick on her cheek.

Disheveled would be an appropriate description, she thought. *No, be honest with yourself. You look liked you've just been fucked.*

She laughed to herself and strolled the rest of the way down the hallway to her room. Turning the key quietly so as not to wake Elio, she opened the door just wide enough to slip inside. As her eyes adjusted to the darkness, she saw her husband still in bed, a symphony of snores cascading from his open mouth.

She breathed deeply, trying to hold on to the bliss she'd just left. Going to the bathroom vanity, she observed her current state with more clarity. She giggled and shook her head at the humor of it all. Turning on the warm water, she wet a washcloth and rubbed the rest of the smeared lipstick from her cheek. Leaving the water running, she discarded her dress, stepped out of her heels, and pulled back her hair. She leaned over the sink, her head hovering over the marble bowl, and lathered and scrubbed her face. Once finished, she spun the knobs of the sink and straightened back up, her face dripping, eyes closed. She reached for the washcloth. But it wasn't where she had left it. Her fingers danced about the counter, searching blindly.

Where was it?

She opened her eyes, the water droplets on her lashes blurring her vision. The vanity lights had been switched off. When had that happened? Had Elio gotten up and turned them off while she was rinsing her face? He was sound asleep, wasn't he? And where the hell had the washcloth gone?

A black gloved hand suddenly shoved the washcloth into her mouth. Vittoria tried to scream, pushing away from her attacker, but the hand towel muffled her cries for help. She swung a fist in defense, but the black glove caught her by the wrist and slammed her arm against the wall in the vanity alcove. Vittoria felt the searing pain of something tearing through her skin as the attacker shoved the blade of a gaudy-looking dagger through her forearm, nailing her in place to the wall. She tried to pull her arm free, but the pain was unbearable. She reached with her free hand to remove the gag from her mouth, but the attacker grabbed her and wrenched her fingers backward until the bones snapped apart in a horrific cacophony.

Her knees gave out, and she braced herself against the counter with her elbow, her forehead resting against the edge. Through her continued screams, she tried to press the washcloth out of her mouth using her tongue, but it was too tightly packed. The gloved hand gently touched the side of her face, as if about to caress her, but then it started pressing, forcing Vittoria's head against the edge of the counter. Her skull felt like it had suddenly been placed in a vise, and someone was spinning it closed. The pressure swelled, and for a moment the pain in her hand and arm disappeared as her focus went solely to her head and the crushing force being applied to it.

A loud crack boomed in her ears. At first she thought it was a gunshot, but quickly realized the sound had come from her own skull. Some part of it had fractured, the first fissure in the dam. She felt as though her cranium was buckling, ready to implode and mash her brain like ground beef.

She wanted to call to Elio. Wanted to beg him to wake up and help her, to save her. And then a terrifying thought arrived: Maybe Elio was already aware she was in trouble. Maybe Elio was the one pressing her head against the counter.

Before she could spend another second wondering, her arm came free of the wall and her attacker released her head, allowing her to slump to the floor. Vittoria laid face down, her body trembling, tears streaming down her face, muffled moans seeping from behind the washcloth gag. Something tugged at her hair, lifting her cheek from the tile, exposing her neck. Her eyes widened, and in that moment, as the dagger's blade pressed against her skin, she once again felt like a terrified little girl.

Chapter 6
Suspicions

Jack awoke to the sound of commotion in the hallway outside his hotel room. He leaned over in bed and checked the time. 9:17 am. His body was already acclimating to vacation life. Normally, he'd have been up with his first cup of coffee in his stomach by this time. Throwing on a robe, he peeked his head out the door, seeing a crowd of guests, hotel staff and a dozen police officers milling about at the far end of the hall.

What the hell's going on?

He stepped into his slippers, then scooped up his room key and dropped it into the pocket of his robe before making his way down toward the crowd. The police and paramedics were swarming around an open guest room, a few of the officers holding the barricade and ushering people away. Jack tried to squeeze past to get a better look at what everyone had come to see, but one of the officers stopped him, placing his hand on Jack's chest and directing him in Italian to return to his room. Jack's suspicious nature urged him to keep trying to see what was happening beyond the open door, but when the officer gave Jack a gentle shove and raised his voice, Jack receded back to his room.

A guest must have had a heart attack, or maybe a stroke, he thought. Planning to ask the concierge about the details later, Jack showered, dressed and headed back out to grab that coffee he was missing. As he waited for the elevator, he could see the crowd of guests and staff members had dispersed, and now only a few police officers in the midst of quiet discussion remained near the now closed door. The presence of lingering police made Jack rethink his initial assumption of a guest with a stroke. Why were they still here? Maybe there had been a robbery? A thief breaking into the room? The guests here certainly had their share of valuables lying about.

The officers caught Jack staring at them, but he didn't shy away, keeping a watchful eye until the elevator arrived to take him down to the main floor.

After ordering up his usual from the barista, Jack posted up on a sofa in the lobby where he had a clear view of the elevators, hoping to glimpse the officers whenever they eventually came down. He heard the quick tapping of dress shoes scurrying across the tile floor behind him and he looked over his shoulder to see the concierge — the one who had given him the tour when he first arrived — hustling from the reception area toward the spa.

"Excuse me," Jack said.

The concierge paused a moment, then started walking again, pretending not to have heard.

"Excuse me, sir," Jack repeated. This time, the concierge stopped, turned to Jack and smiled. "Ah, Mr Ivy! And how are you this morning?"

"Fine. I do have a question for you, though."

The concierge glanced toward the spa as though he were being delayed from seeing to an urgent matter, then walked over to Jack at the sofa and said, "Yes?"

"I'm sorry. What was your name again?"

"Giancarlo, sir."

"Of course. Forgive me. Giancarlo, can you tell me what all that fuss was about earlier with the police?"

"Oh, nothing for you to worry about, Mr Ivy. Please enjoy your day. We have everything under control," Giancarlo said, looking once again toward the spa.

"Well, is everyone alright?"

"Eh, excuse me, Mr Ivy. I apologize, but there is something I really must attend to. Again, nothing to be concerned about." Giancarlo gave a little bow and hurried off. Jack watched him go, even more suspicious now than before.

"May I take that for you, sir?" Jack hadn't even noticed the attendant standing beside him. The man motioned at Jack's empty coffee cup, ready to add it to his collection of abandoned mugs on the tray he held.

Jack nodded and thanked the man, who began to walk away until Jack asked, "Say, you wouldn't know anything about what happened up there on the third floor this morning, would you?"

The attendant bowed his head gravely and responded, "A woman was murdered last night."

Jack sat up to full attention. "Murdered?"

The attendant kept his head low, not making eye contact with Jack, as though it would aid in helping the conversation go unnoticed by his employers. "The wife of that film director. Vittoria Gaeta."

A chill spread across Jack. He shook his head, his brain trying to catch up.

"Her husband must have done it," the attendant continued. "It was clear the man was deranged. The violence in his films?"

The words echoed in Jack's head. He leaned forward over his knees, his hands cradling his head. No, it must be a mistake. She can't be dead. He'd just seen her a few hours earlier. She was perfectly fine until she... Christ. Until she returned to her room after having an affair. Until her husband caught her and...

Jack raised his head to ask another question, but the attendant had sauntered away to resume collecting the discarded dishware from the lobby as though it were a morning like any other. As though a woman hadn't just died. Died because of Jack.

He'd gotten her killed.

It was all his fault. What the hell was he thinking, picking up a married woman at the bar? What the hell did he think would happen when her horror filmmaking husband discovered the truth? And what had Elio said his new movie was about — a man who murders his wife?

A wave of nausea washed over Jack and he rushed to the restroom to vomit, barely getting the stall door open before the contents of his stomach escaped, spewing down into the toilet. He hovered over the bowl, orange strands of bile hanging from his lips, his eyes teary. His knees felt weak, his whole body shaking. He balanced himself on the stall wall to keep from collapsing as flashes from his evening with Vittoria spiraled through his mind.

How could he have let this happen? How could he have done something so... mocking Elio during dinner had all been in good fun. He was just trying to get a rise out of the man. A bit of playful banter, that was all. So why had he taken it so far? Why had he waited at the bar after Vittoria took the drunk man upstairs, hoping she'd return? There was no reason to guess. He knew exactly why. He knew exactly what he was doing. He wanted to fuck her. Plain and simple. He saw a beautiful woman, noticed her interest, and acted on it. No sense in lying to himself. He didn't care that she was married, and maybe it was even more of a turn-on that she was.

And this was the outcome.

A homicide. Jilted husband slays adulterous wife.

Jack had become one of those foolish individuals he got paid to investigate back in Jersey. The secret lover.

He spit loose the dangling strands of saliva from his mouth and wiped his face, not bothering to look at himself in the mirror as he left the restroom. Walking back into the lobby, he saw the attendant, who he had been speaking to moments earlier, standing with Aldo, the resort manager. The attendant pointed at Jack, and as Aldo spotted him, he approached and said, "Mr Ivy. Very sorry to disturb, but the police have asked me to locate you."

"Locate me?" Jack asked.

"They say they have some questions. You can use my office. Please, this way." Aldo swept his hand like a theater usher.

"Questions about what?"

"I couldn't say. They only asked me to find you so that they may speak with you, sir."

Aldo led Jack to a small office near the reception area, invited him to have a seat at the desk, then asked him to wait for the Inspector who he said would be with him momentarily. As Aldo departed, Jack observed the office from the desk chair, noting the many plaques mounted to the wall, awards for the resort's esteemed quality. Hanging beside the door was a framed photograph of Aldo and a dozen other staff members in white uniforms, all standing on one of the Terme del Paradiso balconies overlooking the bay. Jack squinted, trying to make out each of their faces, some of which he recognized from his first few days at the resort.

Sitting atop the desk was a stack of manilla folders. Jack eyed them, curious about their contents. Ignoring his conscious, he flipped open the first file. He scanned through it, quickly identifying it as the reservation details of one of the resort guests — Evelyn Troy. He set it aside and opened the next folder. Another guest file — Dr Roger Simon.

The door swung open and a pair of men in button-up shirts and corduroy suit jackets, who Jack recognized immediately as law enforcement, entered.

"Mr Ivy," the older of the two said, closing the door before setting his espresso saucer down on the desk. "I'm Inspector Righetti." He motioned lazily at the younger man. "My partner, Gallo."

Gallo smiled and gave a half wave, instantly becoming embarrassed at not keeping in line with the stoic demeanor of his partner.

"You're American?" Righetti asked.

"I'm assuming you already know that, based on all these guest files you had the resort manager pull for you," Jack said.

Righetti clocked the open manilla folder on the desk and gave Gallo a look of aggravation, as if it were his partner's responsibility to have put the files back. Then he turned to Jack and asked, "What brings you to Sicily, Mr Ivy?"

"Vacation."

"Vacation. Of course. And what is it you do for work?"

The question stung. A flash of Vittoria's face drowned Jack's mind.

What is it you do when you're not trying to lure women away from their husbands? Jack shook it off. "I'm a photographer," he answered.

"Ah, photography! How relaxing that must be. Nature? Birds? Women? Do share." Righetti took a sip of his espresso.

"Whatever is asked of me."

"Whatever is asked of you? So you're in marketing. Lucrative business. Explains how the resort could cash your check."

"I'm not in marketing."

"Well, don't hold us in anticipation, Mr Ivy. It's such a timely hassle to do checks for foreigners after all. Come on, and save me some agony."

Jack contemplated lying before responding. "I'm a freelance photographer and investigator."

"A private eye! Isn't that what they call it in the States?" Righetti's condescending tone grated on Jack's nerves.

"Some do, yes," Jack said.

"A detective without a badge." Righetti finished his espresso and set the cup back on the saucer.

"That's right."

Righetti sat on the corner of the desk, looking down at Jack. "Well, I know what my salary and pension amounts to, and it's sure nothing to brag about. So tell me, how does a bit-rate investigator afford a room at Terme del Paradiso?"

"My employer fronted the bill."

"Your employer?"

"My latest client, yes. Everything from the plane ticket to the wardrobe."

"Well, isn't that just lovely?" Righetti turned to Gallo. "Isn't that lovely, Gallo? And here I thought employers didn't give a shit about detectives. Hell, my boss must already have a room booked for me come January, after all the work I've put in."

Gallo chuckled. Jack did not.

"You're aware a woman was killed last night?" Righetti asked.

Jack took a moment to answer. "I was told."

"Vittoria Gaeta. Wife of famed director Elio Gaeta."

Jack nodded solemnly.

"She was stabbed. Throat slit." Righetti slid his finger across his neck in a dramatic display. "Absolutely brutal scene."

Jack closed his eyes, the blunt statement hitting him hard.

"Did you know her well?"

"We only met last night," Jack said.

"I'm told you made a bit of a disturbance at her table while she was dining with her husband."

"*Disturbance?* I had a conversation."

"About what?"

"His films."

"You're a fan?"

"No."

"So why were you having a conversation with him about his films, then?"

"I guess I was bored. Thought it would be entertaining."

"And after that?" Righetti asked.

"I went back to my seat at the bar. I didn't speak to Elio again the rest of the evening."

"But you spoke with his wife."

Jack knew the game all too well. All the questions the Inspector was asking were ones he'd already been given answers to. He wasn't looking for information. He was testing to see if Jack would attempt to lie to him.

"That's right," Jack said.

"People saw you sharing drinks with Mrs Gaeta last night, after her husband had retired for the evening. They said the two of you left the lounge together, intimately close." Righetti scrutinized Jack's reaction.

"That's right."

"One of the maids said Mrs Gaeta had her hand down your pants."

Jack breathed deeply, embarrassed. "That's right."

"And then what happened?"

Jack glanced over at Gallo, who was leaning against the closed door like a casual barricade. "We slept together, and after she returned to her room."

"Uh, huh? And what time was that?"

"I don't know," Jack said honestly. "Eleven? Midnight maybe."

"Would you say it's a habit of yours, sleeping with married women, Mr Ivy?"

"To the best of my knowledge, Inspector, she was the first, though I'm not sure it's any of your business."

"Not my business? A woman was sliced apart last night. Do you think that's my business?" Righetti leaned further over the desk toward Jack.

"*That* would be your business. But there's quite a canyon between sex and murder, wouldn't you agree?"

"Not always."

"Am I a suspect?" Jack asked.

"A suspect? Well, I find you suspicious, so yes, I'd say you're a suspect at the moment. You were the last person seen with the victim before her death. You're a fit man. I don't think you'd have much of a challenge stabbing a young woman to death."

"Physically? No. Morally, I'd have quite the issue."

"You're a man of morals, are you? Seems you had no qualms being party to adultery just last night."

"What's your theory here? That I fucked her in my room, then followed her to her husband's and killed her in front of him? He *was* in the room, wasn't he?"

"And how would you know that?"

"Deductive logic."

"Maybe you're a crazed fan. Maybe you wanted to have all the things your favorite film director had, including his wife."

"Or maybe I saw a beautiful woman that I wanted to sleep with, who wanted to sleep with me, and after she left my room, wound up killed, likely by her own jealous husband."

"Jealously? Almost certainly. Perhaps that means you had a hand in her death after all. Maybe if you hadn't fucked her, she'd still be alive."

Jack chewed his cheek, holding back one of a dozen angry responses building in his head. Righetti raised his eyebrows with coy anticipation, and Jack could see disappointment cross his face when he responded calmly. "Unfortunately, that seems rather accurate."

"Very unfortunately, Mr Ivy." Righetti stood and motioned for Gallo to open the door, then waved for Jack to leave.

"That's all?" Jack came around from behind the desk.

"For now, Mr Ivy. Stay close, yes — in case I have any further questions."

"Inspector," Jack said, as he brushed past the two men on his way out. They closed the door behind him, and he lingered just long enough to hear their muffled voices commenting on the interaction.

Aldo approached from the reception desk, his dress shoes tapping softly as he hurried over, and quietly asked, "Everything good, Mr Ivy?"

Jack gave him a look of utter bewilderment. "Good?"

Aldo took a step back, adjusting the lapels of his suit jacket, in a subtle display Jack recognized as sudden social discomfort.

"No," Jack said. "When someone's murdered, I wouldn't say things are very good at all."

Chapter 7
Escape

Jack sat on the edge of his bed, holding the receiver of the red rotary phone, waiting for the call to connect.

"Congressman Baylor's office," a woman's voice answered. "How may I help you?"

"Is the Congressman in? You can tell him it's Jack Ivy. And mention it's urgent, please."

"One moment while I see if he's available."

Jack noticed his leg fidgeting and slapped his hand down upon it, forcibly calming himself.

"Jack?" The Congressman sounded surprised.

"Sorry to bother you, Congressman."

"Debbie said it was urgent. Everything all right?"

"Not in the least. I'm hoping you can get my flight changed. I'd like to come back home."

"Now, hold on. Did something happen? Is there an issue with the room, because I told the manager there—"

"A woman was murdered last night. Right here at the resort."

"Jack!" There was a pause. "Jack." The Congressman's voice morphed into an angry snarl. "What the hell are you talking about? What

the *fuck* are you thinking? You can't be talking to me over the phone about *murders*. Who knows who the hell's listening?"

"Congressman, this is—"

"Jack, people could draw incorrect conclusions. You know, get the wrong idea. The last thing I need is someone thinking I have even the slightest involvement in some international — whatever's happening there has nothing to do with me."

"I didn't say it did. I'm just asking for an earlier flight back."

"An earlier flight? You think that'd be a good look? Fleeing the scene of a — Listen, just forget about it. Okay? Who gives a fuck about some Italian bitch you don't even know, right? Get a massage. Have a couple bottles of wine. Go swim in the ocean, for Christ's sake."

"*Swim in the ocean?* Congressman, I'm trying to tell you—"

"All right then," the Congressman said in his superficial stage voice. "We'll see you next week. Enjoy yourself, Jack."

The line went dead.

Jack set the receiver down in the cradle. He'd gotten his answer. And if he were being honest with himself, it's what he should have expected. Of course, the Congressman wanted nothing to do with it. Why would he touch something like this, knowing the potential repercussions? Could Jack really blame him? The man was just covering his own ass.

It was that Inspector that really had Jack's blood boiling. He'd seen that kind of interrogation tactic many times back home, and knew the lengths law enforcement would go to pin a crime on a scapegoat to save themselves from the work of doing a full investigation. Foreigners were easy targets. Sticking around Sicily was a risk, but without the Congressman's money, Jack had no way of getting back any sooner. The cost of an international plane ticket or even a reservation at another hotel was out of the question. Pipe dreams for his starving bank account. No, he'd have to stay through the week. Hell, it was only a few more days. If he kept his head down, maybe the police would leave him be. They already had their prime suspect in custody, after all.

Jack's mind drifted from thoughts of his own safety, flowing back to the memory of his night with Vittoria.

Thought you might be in town to photograph some Italian models, she had said.

Maybe someday you and I will end up doing a photoshoot together.

He imagined the snap of a crime scene photographer's camera capturing whatever horrible state Vittoria's body had been found in.

Luca's voice echoed, *His new wife. A model, of course. What else for the great Elio Gaeta?*

Jack thought of her mouth, open and bloodstained.

It's called No Mask For Breathing. It's about a famous scuba diver who murders his wife after she's unfaithful to him.

He recalled the soft whoosh of the elevator doors opening while Vittoria's hand was down his pants. The shocked look on the maid's face when she saw them.

What had Vittoria's face looked like when she saw Elio's drunk, vengeful form coming at her? Or maybe she didn't see him coming at all.

Jack wasn't sure what was worse: knowing the gory details of Vittoria's murder, or being forced to make them up in his head. He'd seen enough violence in his life to come up with some awfully gruesome scenarios, and as he sat there on the bed, they all played out in his mind.

He needed to escape, and if that wasn't physically possible at the moment, then he'd need to at least clear his head, rid them of all the ghastly images swirling around inside. And he knew the easiest way to do it.

Chapter 8
How Things Are, How Things Should Be

Silvia watched the circus of police and panicked resort staff from the terrace, the management doing their best to keep everyone calm, while the officers fueled the swelling anxiety with their radios and clomping boots. Rumors had already spread about the beautiful model's murder at the hands of her crazed husband. Silvia thought back to the previous morning when Elio was leering at her fiendishly. He certainly looked the type, and the violent display in the lounge was in line with someone on the verge of physically harming his wife.

She'd also heard rumors about the American, Jack — how he'd had drinks with Vittoria Gaeta late last night, how the two of them left the lounge together. Having a drink wasn't a crime, and even if he'd slept with her, as some rumors suggested, neither was that.

One thing she knew for certain: spending time with someone — even a stranger — so near to their end, was bound to take an emotional toll. It hadn't been that long since Silvia had been in the same boat herself. Loss was powerful. It could send you down dangerous paths. She didn't want to see that happen to Jack. Monitoring the lounge through the window, she hoped to spot him, planning to intercede before he bellied up to the bar and spiraled down an abyss of depression-quenching Bloody Mary's.

It wasn't long before she saw him crossing through the lobby, headed exactly where she knew he'd be going. She walked inside, and just before he reached for a barstool, she called out, "Still around?"

Jack turned, and seeing her, gave a soft smile. "Still around."

"Walk with me," she said.

"I appreciate the invitation, but I'm not sure I'd be good company right now. I was just about to—"

"Walk with me," she repeated.

Jack turned his back to the bar and studied her before asking, "Where?"

THE CORSO UMBERTO IN TAORMINA, the main street of the city, was alive with locals and tourists alike. Silvia led Jack past shops and cafés, churches and historic architecture, the buildings bordering them on both sides, like a protective fortress. They walked together in silence a long way, both pretending to be focused on the sights, both of their minds somewhere very different. Finally Jack said, "I didn't hurt her. I know that's what some people are saying, but I didn't. I could never in a million years—"

"If I thought you were a murderer, I wouldn't have asked you to go for a walk with me." She pat him gently on the back.

He nodded. "I suppose that's true."

"Are you hungry? There are a lot of great restaurants around here."

"I'm not sure I could keep anything down."

"A coffee then?"

"I'm good for now, I think. If you'd like something, I'm happy to stop with you."

"No, I'm good as well." She struggled to keep the conversation going, to distract him even a few more moments from the thought of Vittoria's death.

"You told me you're here in Sicily to reunite with your father. Does he live nearby?"

"Closer to Randazzo. I told him I'd call him when I'm ready to meet. I guess I'm still working up the nerve."

"How long has it been since you've seen him?"

"About six years. He didn't approve of the man I married."

"You're—" Jack slowed his pace. "I didn't realize."

"My husband passed," she said, still walking.

"I'm very sorry to hear that." Jack sped up to keep from falling behind.

"He was sick for a long while. It gave me time to come to terms with the reality. Though sometimes I wonder if it would have been easier if his death had been sudden."

Silvia noticed a subtle twitch in Jack's face, as if the idea of sudden death had immediately thrown his mind back to where she was trying to keep it from returning.

"But he was a good man," she said. "I'll always cherish the memories I have of him. And while he's not here for me now, he left me the protection of money."

"He was well off?"

"His family acquired a lot after the war. Built themselves up. Even left me a palazzo. I'm very fortunate."

"And now you're trying to build something back of your own."

"If my father isn't a complete bastard, yes." She paused before saying, "It would be nice to be around family again."

A whistle echoed from beside them. They looked to see three men catcalling Silvia in Italian. Jack turned and faced them, but Silvia grabbed him by the arm and forced him to keep walking.

"Come on," she said.

"Those men—"

"Don't get so defensive. It happens all the time."

"That doesn't make it okay." Jack glanced back at the men, two of them laughing, the third still ogling Silvia's backside.

"How things are, and how things should be, are always so far apart. I'm sure it's no different in America."

"In America, catcalling a lady on the street is a good way to get your teeth knocked out."

"Do you want to fight them? Teach them some manners?" She smirked, keeping her arm looped around Jack's.

He couldn't help but grin. "Maybe I do."

"Oh really? You think you can handle all three?"

"I'd give it my best shot."

"Yes, but I'd be the one having to help you all the way back to the resort after they kicked your ass. Maybe you should save the tough guy antics for when you get back home. It'll spare me the heavy lifting."

Jack chuckled, and Silvia hugged him around the shoulders as they continued walking, knowing she was finally making some headway in pulling him out of the dark void. As they passed by the window of a small bakery, she stopped him and pointed inside at the baker piping filling into a fresh cannoli.

"Here. This is when they are best, right after they've been filled," she said.

"Cannolis?"

"You've never had a cannoli until you've had a cannoli in Sicily."

"I thought you weren't hungry," Jack said playfully.

"Cannolis don't count as eating. Enjoying a cannoli is... like an activity." She forced him inside and ordered a pair, then watched enthusiastically as Jack bit into the dessert. He nodded in approval.

"I'm right?"

"You're right," he admitted.

"Fresh ricotta cream. Pistachios." She took a bite, closing her eyes as if every neuron in her brain were firing at once, then sighed with satisfaction. She smiled at the baker as he filled more cannolis to put into the display case, and said, "Grazie. Perfetto."

Jack mirrored Silvia, one hand holding the cannoli, the other acting as a tray to catch any of the buttery flakes of the pastry shell that may attempt to escape. The awkward humor of it all was palpable, both of their mouths full, communicating their enjoyment to one another through facial expressions alone. Silvia finished hers first, quickly checking for crumbs or smeared ricotta cream at the edges of her mouth with the tip of her thumb, then took Jack by his tray hand and piloted him out of the bakery, back onto the Corso Umberto.

"Okay, *now* I'm ready for an espresso," Silvia said. "Always need an espresso after a cannoli."

Still chewing his last bite, Jack gestured back the way they had come. "There was a little café right back there."

"Not that one." Her arm slid back around Jack's as she guided him further along. The street opened up into a square with a fountain at its center and a looming cathedral at the far end. Their destination, a busy café with a wide terrace facing the cathedral, sheltered its guests from the sun with an array of crimson umbrellas. They chose a table in the shade and Silvia ordered a pair of espressos.

"Have you been to the spa yet?" she asked Jack.

"I went yesterday, actually."

"How was it?"

"I have little to compare it to. It was my first massage. Don't frequent those types of places in Jersey. But the masseuse seemed to know what she was doing. I felt amazing the rest of the day."

"I still need to see it. Maybe I'll do that when we get back."

Jack picked up the menu the waiter had left, but set it back down when he realized everything was written in Italian. Silvia smirked. "Would you like me to help you pick something out?"

"I should have taken a class on Italian before I flew out here," Jack said.

Silvia scanned through the menu, hailed the waiter and placed an order. She handed the menu to the waiter who thanked her and strolled away. When Silvia turned back to Jack, she caught him staring at her mouth. His eyes quickly returned to her.

"You like when I speak in Italian?"

"It's a beautiful language," he said. "What did you order?"

Silvia made him wait for the food to arrive before giving a description of each item, presenting it to him the way a master chef might indulge his honored guests.

"They call Sicily *God's kitchen.* We take food from the mountains, the fields, and the sea. Everything fresh, everything Sicilian, which is to say a blend of all the cultures who have made their mark on the island throughout history."

"So you're trying to tell me it's not just Italian food," Jack said, looking at the three dishes the waiter set down in front of them.

"Sicilian food and Italian food are two different things," Silvia explained. "These are Sicilian. You won't find these recipes anywhere else in the country." She gestured to the plate closest to Jack, a golden-brown, cone-shaped item. "Arancino. Fried rice ball stuffed with a creamy veal sauce, mozzarella and mushrooms."

Jack cut into it and took a bite. "That's really good," he said, pointing at the arancino with the tip of his knife, his mouth still full.

Silvia swapped the plate with the next dish, this one a pasta topped with a colorful array of vegetables. "Pasta alla Norma. Aubergines, ricotta, basil, tomatoes."

Jack scooped a bit of everything onto his fork and enjoyed the aroma before taking a bite. He nodded and said, "Very good. Aubergines?"

"Eggplant," she said.

"Eggplant. So it's eggplant and pasta."

"That's a boring way of describing it, but yes. It's eggplant and pasta."

Jack chuckled and went to scoop up another bite, but Silvia pulled the plate away and slid the third and final dish in front of him. "Frutti di mare," she said. "Fruit of the sea." It was a dark brown pasta with a bouquet of pink tentacles at its center.

"Fruit of the sea," Jack repeated.

"It's the squid's ink that gives the pasta its black coloring. Spaghetti al nero di seppia."

Jack stared at it apprehensively, the tiny curled tentacles like a rose atop the nest of otherworldly-looking noodles. "Squid. I'm not sure if I'm—"

"Live a little, Jack."

As he worked up the courage to try the seafood, the waiter returned with two glasses of white wine. They toasted to good company and Jack finally tried the pasta al nero, admitting it was better than he expected. It was then Silvia allowed him to have more of the arancino. They shared the three dishes, finishing nearly every bite, the conversation casually flowing from one topic to the next as if the two had known one another for years.

The day passed, and before either had realized the time, the sun fell behind the mountains. Along their trek back to Terme del Paradiso, Silvia steered them down a path to the beach, removing her shoes, feeling the white sand beneath her feet. Jack did the same and rolled the cuffs of his pants up around his calves.

"I can't imagine not living near water like this." Silvia held her dress to keep it from touching the sand as they walked.

"It's quite amazing," Jack said.

"Do you live near the ocean?"

"Close. But the beaches in Jersey aren't anything like this."

"No? Are you envious of our—"

Before Silvia could finish her sentence, Jack pulled her in close to his chest. She watched his eyes trace her face, honing in on...

She kissed him, then pulled back to get his reaction. He paused only briefly before they kissed again, this time longer, deeper. As they melted into one another, his hand slid down along her hip and she said, "Forget the spa. Let me show you my room."

Unbothered by the potential voyeurism, Silvia left the curtains open, allowing the evening glow to illuminate the otherwise tenebrous suite. Her clothes mingled with Jack's on the floor as the two of them stumbled into the bedroom.

Her tongue was in his mouth as she moved his hands to her breasts. Forcing him flat on his back, she kissed his chest, then his naval, then slid down further. Keeping eye contact with him, she ensured he watched as she began stroking. She grinned seductively when her tongue made his body shiver. One of his hands reached for her, grazing her hair. Needing no guidance, she grabbed him by the wrist and forced his hand away. Then she took him in, and she could feel him twitch as he took a sudden breath. Her lips tightened, her tongue circling, massaging. As soon as she tasted the first escape of flavor, she released him, not yet ready to force him to climax.

Her lips found his again, and she moved atop him, her breasts in his face. Raising higher, she moved her hips above his head and he strained towards her. She felt the warmth of his tongue inside her and she arched her back, her palms flat against the wall behind the headboard. Grinding gently, she kept his arms pinned beneath her shins, holding him in position until she was satisfied.

Once she freed him, Jack slapped her ass and Silvia yelped playfully. As he turned her over, she giggled, stretching out on her stomach. He knelt behind and grabbed her hips, lifting her ass higher, using his knee to spread her legs further apart. She felt him move into her. His teeth found her shoulder and the pressure of his bite made her gasp. She reached back, grabbing his ass cheek, forcing him to continue fucking her, not letting go until the thrusts became so aggressive that she needed both forearms on the bed for support.

Silvia knew she had succeeded in taking Jack's mind off the death of Vittoria Gaeta. But *her* thoughts dwelled heavily on the dead woman.

She wondered, *Had Vittoria been in this exact position the previous night? Had Jack fucked her just like this? Was it the last ounce of enjoyment she had before her blood painted the walls of Terme del Paradiso?*

Chapter 9
The Skills Of Illaria Conti

Illaria Conti learned her knife skills from her grandfather. As early as four years old, he was teaching her the proper way to hold an edged blade, how to cut meat, trim fat, chop and dice vegetables. He told her that all chefs have a good scar or two, and also a good story or two of how they received each of those scars. Some came from being distracted. Some came from rushing and ignoring proper etiquette. But most came from using a knife that was too dull. Safety, he would say, was the most important part of the culinary arts. Food safety, and safety for one's self and those around them.

Her grandfather was a restaurant manager, and would often tell her she had better skill sets than many of his cooks. He let her start with soft foods — berries, avocados — and then gradually moved her up to denser items like onions and pork. He taught her to scramble eggs. He taught her how to avoid burns. *Control, control, control*, he would say.

As far as mentors came, Illaria could not have asked for anyone better than her grandfather. Not only was he knowledgeable, he was also patient and kind, and with her father gone — having committed suicide after the war — her grandfather was also her caretaker. She loved him more than she had loved anything her entire life, and when he passed just before she applied for a position at the five star resort of Terme del Paradiso, she felt as though his spirit had been with her during her stage in the kitchen.

Above all odds, she got herself a job as a prep cook, working under the esteemed executive chef Francesco Berlusconi and his team, who tested her resolve daily. She had a test coming up in a few weeks, an opportunity to move from prep cook to cook. That's where she would get to work on the dishes, alongside the true professionals. She was dreading the challenge, though she knew she had the skill set from all her years of practice and her grandfather's tutelage.

But her current focus that night was her prep work, to get the list done for the real cooks who would prepare the meals for all the posh guests at the resort the following day. The chef always made her work the overnight shift, and it was her job to ensure everything was ready for the sous chef in the morning to fire breakfast. For part of the night, another prep cook accompanied her, but after 10pm he would leave, and Illaria would be alone in the deep secluded kitchen.

Most nights the isolation wouldn't have bothered her, but after news had spread of the model that was murdered the previous evening, she had to admit she was a bit on edge. The squeal of the service door swinging open startled her, and she nearly dropped the chef's knife she was using to cut carrots.

Luca, the bartender, gave her a humorously apologetic expression as he walked in with a pair of full shot glasses. "Sorry, sorry. Didn't mean to scare you."

Illaria set the knife down on the cutting board and leaned against the prep table. "Shouldn't you be gone by now?"

"I've been off the clock for a bit, just needed a drink," he said as he set the two shot glasses down between them. "And a shot to chase it."

"If Sergio knew you were back here, he'd have your ass," she said.

"Are you going to tell him?"

Illaria grinned and picked up the shot glass. She had enjoyed the nightly banter with Luca ever since he'd first worked up the courage to speak with her. He was charming, and undeniably good looking. Two handy traits for bartending, she imagined.

"We'll just have to see," she said. They toasted and threw back their shots. As Luca smiled at her coyly, she could read his every thought. She knew he loved flirting with her, always throwing her a compliment or two when she took her breaks, often finding her after his shifts for a couple minutes of impish repartee to keep the sexual tension elevated.

"How was the staff back here after the news broke?"

"Quieter than out there, I'm sure," she said, nodding toward the lounge.

"Yes, quite the gossipy crowd tonight. But can't blame anyone for being a bit heightened, right?" He scooped up the empty shot glasses. "Speaking of which, can I interest you in one more of these? Help keep any spooky thoughts out tonight?"

The offer was tempting. A single shot wasn't going to hurt, but two was a different story. Two led to three, and three to four, and four or more meant all that knife safety would be out the window. The chef would walk in to find an absolute mess, with one of her fingers chopped off and the carrots marinating in a bath of intoxicated blood.

It was a bit of an exaggeration, she knew, but the stakes certainly felt that high. Regardless of how much she wanted to spend a night drinking with Luca — and God did that sound good — she wasn't stupid enough to throw away everything her grandfather had helped her achieve for an evening with some cocky bartender.

"Not tonight," she said.

"Uh huh," Luca replied, already having predicted her answer.

And before she knew what she was saying, she countered with, "But I'm off Monday."

Luca raised an eyebrow, and Illaria waited apprehensively for his response. Had she misread his flirtatious behavior? Had it all been in jest to pass the time? Of course. He's just a co-worker making frivolous conversation. Nothing more. How foolish of her. He never actually wanted more than that. He didn't honestly—

"Dinner?" he offered. The moment it took him to respond felt like an eternity, but time seemed to return to normal at the utterance of that simple word.

"Yeah. Yes. Dinner would be nice." She gripped the edge of the prep table so he wouldn't see her hands trembling with excitement.

He smiled brightly, all sense of arrogance evaporating. "Okay then." He took a step back and paused. Illaria thought he might lean in and kiss her, but had that been his plan, he quickly reassessed and instead gave a comical bow and said, "Till Monday then, milady."

She grinned and shook her head, then picking up the knife, she pointed it at him and said, "Don't make me regret it."

"I'll pick out a good spot. I know you're a snob when it comes to fine cuisine."

"*Snob?*" She scoffed and threw a slice of carrot, pegging him in the chest as he backed away.

Luca laughed, putting his hands out defensively. "Snob isn't a bad thing. You're cultured. That's all I'm saying."

"*Goodnight*, Luca."

"Monday," he said.

"Monday."

He nodded and walked out of the kitchen, then leaned back in through the door, and repeated once more, "Monday." He rapped on the door, then disappeared.

Illaria could feel the heat of her blushing cheeks as she went back to chopping the carrots. She couldn't quite believe what had just transpired. Was that all it took? Just asking him herself? She should have done it months ago.

When she finished with the carrots, she heaved the full container onto a cart and rolled it across the kitchen to the walk-in cooler. As usual, she had to yank hard to get the door to open, revealing the frigid interior. She wheeled the cart across the corrugated threshold and stocked the container beside the rest of the produce she'd already prepped. The door closed behind her, softly sealing Illaria inside. Every night, going inside the cooler made her think of what it must be like onboard a submarine. The cold metal walls and floor, the whirr of the cooling fan drowning out all sound from outside. It was surprisingly tranquil.

She pulled down half a dozen bundles of asparagus and stacked them on the cart before collecting a few cases of strawberries, then she backed into the door, shoving it open with her ass, and pulled the cart out. As she unloaded the produce onto the prep table, she wondered where Luca might take her to dinner. There was Malfatti's, a boutique seafood restaurant she'd heard recommended a lot, though she'd never been herself. Pigozzi's was always good. No matter how often she'd eaten there, she never grew tired of it. Maybe he'd take her *there*. She supposed it didn't matter, really. It wasn't about the food; it was about seeing Luca... outside of work.

She washed the strawberries and set them out to dry as she cleaned the asparagus. With impressive speed, she chopped the spears into perfectly symmetrical lengths, her knife moving with confident ease. Her thoughts drifted back to her conversation with Luca. He'd almost kissed her, hadn't he? She knew that's what he was about to do. So why didn't he just do it? *She* should have leaned in and kissed *him*. But maybe that would have been too bold. She'd already been the one to initiate the date, after all. She didn't want to make him feel—

To hell with that, she thought. *It's probably the reason he's interested in me to begin with. I don't shy away. I know what I want and I go after it, be it a job, a promotion, or a man. I don't—*

A metallic twang echoed from somewhere deep inside the kitchen. Illaria stretched up on her tiptoes to look over the two-tiered prep table, expecting to see Luca or another staff member.

No one was there.

"Hello?" She waited for a response that never came. "*Hello?*" The kitchen was pin drop-silent. All the unease she had felt before her conversation with Luca immediately swelled back into place. Gripping the handle of the chef's knife, she kept her sights fixed in the direction of the mysterious noise. Someone had bumped against something back there, maybe knocked a pan into another, or hit a pot with something metal, a serving spoon... or a knife.

On any other night, her thought process would have seemed silly. But not tonight. Not after a guest was murdered. Illaria moved backward slowly until she felt the wall beside the walk-in cooler. Without diverting her eyes, she reached blindly for the knife rack mounted on the wall beside her head. Her fingers fondled across the assorted handles. She knew each of them by the feel and size, eventually selecting the fillet knife. With a blade in each hand, she stood ready should any psychopath emerge from some hidden crevice of the kitchen.

She considered calling for help, considered screaming.

But what if she was wrong? What if she *was* alone in the kitchen and whatever staff member that came running to help ended up telling the chef about the timid prep cook who was too afraid to work by herself? She would not give him any reason to doubt her. She'd done well to let her skills speak for themselves. That wasn't going to change now. If there *was* someone in the kitchen with her, someone who meant her harm, she'd scream out for help when she confirmed it. But until then, until she knew it wasn't just her imagination running wild, she'd wait in solidarity with her knives.

A minute passed. Then five. And Illaria felt extremely foolish standing like a Viking warrior wielding dual blades. She laughed quietly at herself and her body loosened. Returning to the prep table, she moved on to the strawberries. She removed the tops, then sliced them into quarters before piling them into a Cambro container. When she'd finished all the cases, she loaded the container onto the cart and began wheeling it back over to the walk-in cooler.

She stopped halfway, then doubled back and grabbed the chef's knife off the table.

"Just in case," she said to herself as she set it on the cart. Just because she had a job to do didn't mean she was going to let her guard down.

Once again she pulled the door open and pushed the cart inside the cooler. The container was heavy, but years of lifting and stocking product had left her in good physical shape.

The gentle hiss of the seal let her know the door had closed behind her. She reached for a case of tomatoes on the top shelf of the rack, her fingers grazing the edge of the cardboard box. She stretched further up on her tiptoes again until her fingers could curve around the lip and pulled it towards her. Her other hand supported the bottom of the case as she lowered it down onto the cart, then she grabbed a second case and stacked it atop the first.

The unmistakable chime of metal tapping against metal resonated from behind her. Goose flesh raised on her arm as she realized there was someone else inside the cooler with her. She turned toward the door. A figure in a dark hat and oversized raincoat stood before her, his face indiscernible, obscured by a sort of thin black mask. In his hand: a knife, the tip casually clinking against the nearest shelving unit.

Illaria screamed!

A gloved hand reached to cover her mouth, but she shoved the masked figure back, then grabbed the case of tomatoes, using it as a shield just as the vicious-looking blade slashed out at her. It sliced easily through the cardboard, puncturing a tomato, spraying the juice across Illaria's face. The rest tumbled out of the box, bouncing and rolling between her feet.

Again, the blade came for her. She dodged out of the way just in time, the blade twanging off the top of the metal cart, the vibration rattling Illaria's forgotten chef's knife.

My knife!

She caught it by the handle just before it slid off, and with the speed of a fencing master, she swung it in an upward curve at her attacker's face, the tip of the chef's knife nicking the brim of his hat as he leaned away.

With her free hand, Illaria grabbed the cart by the handle and spun it to create a barrier, then she sprinted further into the cooler, turning down the second row of shelving. There was no need to take an inventory of things she could use for defense. Illaria knew the cooler better than anyone. Every case of watermelon, every tub of butter, every container of raw chicken. She reached the end of the aisle and positioned herself at the rear of the cooler, bobbing back and forth to see down both rows.

The masked figure shoved the cart out of the way and stood facing

Illaria from the other end of the walk-in. Again, Illaria screamed for help. Why hadn't anyone come to check on her? There were still people just outside the kitchen in the lounge. Guests. Co-workers. Hadn't any of them heard?

Of course not.

The walk-in cooler was a soundproof chamber. You couldn't hear anything, even if you were standing just outside of it. There was no chance any of those people out there in the lounge would hear her screams.

"Come any closer and I'll cut your fucking head off!" Illaria held the chef's knife up in front of her face for him to see.

The masked figure held his own knife up in response, giving Illaria her first clear look at it. The cruciform blade was nearly eight inches in length, the metal worn, with a bit of rust speckled across it. Its pommel was curved at the end like a pistol, and it bore a cross guard with ball finials. This was no kitchen knife. It was a military dagger.

...One that seemed strangely familiar.

His head tilted, examining his surroundings, pausing a moment and focusing on the closest light bulb. Then it swiveled back toward Illaria's direction and somehow, even through the black mask, Illaria could tell he was smiling.

He approached one of the shelving racks, grabbing hold of the top shelf while stepping up onto the bottom. Reaching toward the ceiling, he stabbed the bulb. Illaria could hear the shattered glass raining down as an entire section of the cooler fell into darkness, and the masked figure disappeared.

Illaria looked up at the ceiling. Only one bulb remained, midway between her and her attacker. She heard the moan of the shelving unit, assuming he was climbing back down. Steady footsteps approached. The masked figure appeared once more, coming into the light beneath the final bulb. Illaria moved into the second aisle, using the shelving rack and all the product boxes stacked upon it as a protective wall. Through the gaps she could see him select a small, heavy box the size of a brick from the shelf, then he hurled it up at the lightbulb. It exploded, sending glass shards and tiny black sesame seeds sprinkling everywhere.

The shadows absorbed them both.

Illaria was blind.

She shoved a large case of melons across the shelf toward the last place she'd seen the masked figure standing. She heard it land, the melons bouncing and rolling across the cold, slick floor. Then she felt the whoosh of something fly past her head, and from her knowledge of the cooler, knew it to be a case of romaine. It landed beside her, and before she could move, something blunt hit her in the face, knocking her backward against the shelving unit along the cooler wall. She caught the cardboard box full of peppers as she stumbled back, then tossed it aside, trying not to trip over the case of lettuce in the process.

She contemplated running for the door. Maybe she could reach it before the figure did. Maybe she could get out and lock him inside.

Illaria made a mad dash.

With every step she took, her mind honed in on her memory of the cooler. The shelving, the boxes, even the over-sized container that the sous chef always placed unsafely on the bottom shelf at shin height. She dodged past it with ease. The door was only a few more meters away. She could hear her attacker's frantic footsteps chasing after her, but she had a strong lead.

She was going to make it.

She was going to get out and lock the son of a bitch inside.

The door was only—

Her foot stepped down into something soft and wet, and her leg slid out from beneath her. As she fell, she reached out wildly for anything to regain her balance. Her shoulder hit the prep cart, and she landed hard, her head smacking off the tomato slathered floor.

The footsteps dissipated. The only sound Illaria could hear was the whirr of the cooling fan, and the high pitch ringing in her ears. Her fingers fondled the back of her head, praying she wouldn't feel her brain squeezing out through a crack in her skull. Her hair was wet, but it wasn't warm like blood. Tomato juice.

Still gripping the chef's knife, she quietly pulled herself up onto her knees. Something brushed across her face, some kind of material. And Illaria realized the figure was standing right beside her.

The knife was dull.

She felt it snag on her skin, tearing into her just below her shoulder joint. She screamed and swung the chef's knife up into the pitch black; the blade catching something, slicing through the same material that had caressed her face. Illaria heard a gasp escape from beneath her attacker's mask and the dull knife quickly retracted from her flesh. She swung again, then jabbed, neither attack finding anything but air.

Light flared in Illaria's eyes as the cooler door flew open, and she raised her arm like a shield. Her attacker ran out, and for the fleetest of moments, Illaria thought she had won. Then the door squeezed back closed — the hiss of the seals no longer a soothing sound — and she was plunged back into darkness.

She charged at the door, throwing her entire body weight against it. But it didn't budge. She yanked the handle, and when it only gave a millimeter of movement, she knew immediately the pin had been slid into the lock on the outside.

Christ.

"*Help!*" Banging on the door, kicking and pounding against it, hoping someone — anyone — would hear and come to her aid, she screamed till she was hoarse.

It was only then that the chill of the cooler settled into her. She'd been filled with so much adrenaline that she'd hardly noticed it. But now, the temperature of the cooler suddenly seemed much more urgent.

Three degrees celsius. That's what it was set at. As long as it was above freezing, she figured she could survive long enough for someone to show up in the morning and find her. The sous chef. He was always the first one in. Illaria had never wanted to see him as badly as she did now, standing there in the darkness, shivering... bleeding.

Fuck.

How had she forgotten about the gaping hole below her shoulder? She had to patch herself up, or she'd bleed out long before the sous chef could arrive. Unbuttoning her chef's coat, she used her knife to cut her undershirt off midriff, then used the material to fashion a bandage, using her teeth to cinch it tightly over the wound. Her fingers traced over it blindly, hoping it would suffice until morning.

She searched the lowest shelf for a sturdy container, finding a case of broccoli. Pulling it out, she sat cross-legged atop it, keeping herself from making any further contact with the cold floor. She rested her arms across her knees and closed her eyes, focusing on controlling her breathing. There was likely more than enough oxygen inside the cooler, but she didn't see any sense in risking it. The less excited her breathing was, the slower she'd burn through it. She grinned as she imagined what she must look like, sitting there atop the vegetables in a meditative pose. Her sense of confidence crawled back, and she assured herself she'd survive.

It was all going to be okay.

Chapter 10
The Man With The Blue Eyes

It had been a few years since Jack had awakened beside a naked woman. That's not to say he hadn't slept with his share during that time, but they usually left after the act... after he paid. His job didn't afford him much time for a social life, too busy sleeping during the day, photographing persons-of-interest at night. He needed to get his needs met somehow, and New Jersey's working girls were the easiest way to do that.

Doing his best not to wake Silvia, he sat up and leaned against the ornate headboard, his head still hazy from the wine. He admired the shape of her body beneath the thin sheet, her hair fanned out across the pillow as though meticulously arranged by a fashion photographer trying to capture a cover page shot. Glancing around the room, the evidence of the passionate evening transported him back in time. Their clothes, hastily stripped off, like bread crumbs leading toward the bed. The bottle of Sangiovese delivered by room service, now empty and lying on its side. Jack grinned as he recalled Silvia tripping over her heels on her way to take a piss. He'd jumped out of bed to help her up, both of them laughing, Silvia shoving him away to escape to the toilet. The window, like a picture frame holding the world's beauty prisoner. Silvia had stood before it in her robe, Jack cradling her from behind, both of them gazing out at the reflection of the stars dancing across silent waves. Congressman Baylor hadn't embellished the grandeur of the scenery one bit.

Defused by the sheer curtains, it was now the sun's turn to awe. It warmed Silvia's face, delicately luring her from her sleep. Jack watched as she lay for a beat, entranced by the window and all that existed beyond it. Then she rolled over toward him, looking up with squinting eyes.

"Good morning," Jack said.

Silvia groaned and stretched, then pulled herself in tight against him. "You talk in your sleep, you know?"

"That right?" Jack asked. "And what is it I was saying?"

"I couldn't really make it out. Just a bunch of mumbling."

"Mumbling? I'll have you know, Jack Ivy is no mumbler. I don't mumble when I'm awake, nor when I'm sleeping. I speak clearly and to the point at all times."

Jack could feel a smile form on Silvia's face as her cheek rested against his chest. "Oh yes, you're consistently proper and professional, Mr Ivy," she said.

"That's right," Jack concurred.

"Quite the professional last night, to be sure."

Jack grinned. "What do you say we try out the spa today?"

"That sounds wonderful," Silvia said and sat up. "But I think today's the day I'm going to force myself to meet with my father."

"Good for you. Get it out of the way so you can enjoy the rest of your stay."

"When I get back, I'd like to see you again."

"I'll be around," Jack assured her with his staple line. "In the meantime, you have a phone call to make." He squeezed her thigh and gave her a kiss, then got out of bed and began collecting his clothes.

"I could make time for a coffee before I go," she offered. "Downstairs in an hour?"

Jack pulled up his pants. "Absolutely."

～

It was more than enough time to shower, shave, and pick out his next outfit. He took the elevator down, surprised to still see a police presence, this time congregating near the lounge. Through the sea of uniforms, Inspector Righetti in his earth tone suit was easy to spot. He locked eyes with Jack, then excused himself from the conversation he was in the middle of to make his way across the lobby.

"Mr Ivy," Righetti called. Jack sighed, waiting for the Inspector to traverse the distance. "Mr Ivy, I'd like a moment of your time."

"And what can I do for the police *today*, Inspector?" Jack's annoyance bled through every word.

"Oh, apologies for interrupting your morning, sir. How thoughtless of me," Righetti shot back with oozing sarcasm. "It's just that there was another attack last night, and wouldn't you know it, happened right here at the resort again."

Confusion extinguished Jack's frustration. "Another—"

"Attack. That's right. The night cook. She's lucky to be alive. And before you make a joke about the food not being *that* bad, save yourself the self-congratulatory pat on the back because I've already heard it half a dozen times from you people this morning."

"The cook — that's horrible. Is she all right?"

"I wouldn't say 'all right,' but she's still breathing, and that's something."

"Jesus Christ."

"And where were *you* last night, Mr Ivy?"

"I — I was here. At the resort."

"Drinking in the lounge again?"

"What? No. No, I was—"

Righetti's thick eyebrows raised, impatiently awaiting an answer.

"I spent the night with a friend," Jack finally said.

Righetti grinned. "*Another* friend. This one married too?"

Jack's jaw clenched. "Listen here—"

"This friend, you were with her all night?"

Jack glanced over at the other police officers milling about near the lounge. "Yeah."

"And what is her name? I'm going to need to speak with her."

Jack looked back at Righetti. "What for?"

"Part of proving you have an alibi is me speaking to them to confirm it. I'd assumed you were at least familiar with the process, considering you're an amateur detective and all. Her name?"

Jack let the slight roll off his shoulder. "Silvia."

"Silvia what? Surely you know your friend's surname."

Jack scoffed. This cop would fit right in back in Jersey, he thought. They're all so tough, hiding behind the badge. He looked Righetti straight in the eye. "Pasquale."

"Very good. And she's a guest here?"

"What else would she be?"

"Perhaps a staff member? Maybe one of Sicily's ladies of the night? I can't presume to know your inclinations, Mr Ivy."

"She's a guest," Jack said.

"A guest. Good. That will make things easier. Is she here now?"

"In her room."

"And that's where you spent the night? Or were the two of you in *your* room?"

"We were in hers," Jack said.

"Very good." Righetti patted Jack on the arm, then lightly squeezed his bicep. "Oh. Quite the arms on you. Spend time in the gym?"

"Not much."

"Enough though," Righetti said.

"Enough for what, Inspector? Say what you mean to say."

Righetti chuckled. "Enough to do some damage, Mr Ivy. Let's hope Ms Pasquale can attest to your whereabouts last night." He moved as if he were going to walk away, then turned back and said, "Or is it *Mrs* Pasquale? I know how you enjoy the company of married women."

"You can ask her when you speak with her, Inspector."

From across the lounge, Righetti's partner, Gallo, called for him in Italian. Righetti shouted back and left Jack without another word, heading to see what his flustered partner required.

With the Inspector no longer staring him down, Jack realized his hand had been shaking nervously. He quickly clutched the back of the sofa to steady it, not wanting anyone to see. He knew he was innocent, but that wouldn't keep the police from pressing him. Righetti had made his disdain for Jack all too clear, and Jack could see himself through the Inspector's suspicious eyes. Jack was a foreigner, had questionable morals, and threw in his lot with the wealthy elite like the rest of the resort guests. Those were three strikes against him. If the son of a bitch wanted to put Jack in his crosshairs and pull the trigger, it wouldn't take much more convincing to do so.

"It seems as though blood flows continuously here in Sicily," a voice said from behind Jack. He turned to see the same attendant from the previous morning, once again collecting used coffee cups. "Sometimes it's from the veins you want, other times it's not. Accepting that is the only way one seems able to survive."

Jack stared at the man, who failed to look over at him and instead kept his head down as he placed another cup on his tray.

"Do you know something about all this, friend?" Jack asked.

"About death? I know far too much, I'm afraid. We're old friends, he and I."

The words chilled Jack's marrow. "Yeah? That so?" he asked, cautiously keeping his distance. He read the name tag pinned beside the attendant's lapel. "Marco?"

The man, Marco, finally faced Jack, his striking blue eyes unblinking as though it were a contest. He looked neither solemn nor incensed, his expression a stoic display.

The clicking of heels preceded Silvia's voice. "Jack." He turned to her as she approached from the elevator. She was focused on the police over near the lounge as she asked, "What happened?"

Jack waited until she was close enough to answer quietly. "Another attack. A cook this time."

"*What?* When?"

"Last night. The police just questioned me, wanted to know where I was."

"*You?* They're relentless! You were with me all night. I'll tell them."

"I think you're going to have to," Jack said. "The Inspector said he wants to hear it straight from your mouth."

When Jack looked back over his shoulder, Marco had vanished. He glanced around, finally spotting him across the lobby.

"You don't think this attack is somehow connected to Vittoria's murder, do you?" Silvia asked. "Do the police still have Elio Gaeta in custody?"

But Jack didn't hear her. His sights were fixated on Marco, watching as the man disappeared through a STAFF ONLY door with his full tray of cups. As he replayed the words Marco had said over and over in his head, he couldn't shake the image of the man's unnervingly blue eyes.

"Jack?" Silvia said.

He turned back to her. "What? Sorry."

"I asked if the police still had Elio Gaeta locked up."

"I don't know. I didn't ask, and even if I did, I'm sure the Inspector wouldn't say."

"Two attacks in two nights? What the hell is going on?" Silvia leaned into him, and he wrapped an arm around her shoulder. "I can't think on it anymore, Jack. It's just too horrible."

She was right. It was horrible. *Beyond* horrible. But Jack wasn't ready to put it aside. His investigation had just begun.

Chapter 11
J&B On The Rocks

After Inspector Righetti finished interviewing Silvia to confirm Jack's story, she recounted the conversation with Jack to ease his mind. As the day was getting on, they skipped the coffee so she could make the trip to meet with her father. Jack saw her off as she departed the resort by taxi. He stood on the front steps, leaning against the baroque railing, debating how to spend his day, which had begun with such unexpected horror.

What had the Congressman said? Get a massage, have a couple drinks, and go for a swim?

It suddenly sounded like brilliant advice. He strolled in through the reception area, across the lobby toward the spa entrance on the eastern side. He inquired about booking a massage appointment, but the receptionist informed him that because of the overwhelming amount of guests who flooded her desk that morning, there were no openings for the rest of the day. She invited him to enjoy the sauna, the stream room or the indoor bathhouse, as those did not require an appointment. He declined the proposal and instead returned to his room, where he collected his camera and loaded a roll of film.

Upon his balcony he stood, snapping photograph after photograph of the bay, an unparalleled sight if he'd ever seen one. Through the viewfinder, he traced the coastline, yachts floating over the cresting waves, rocking gently to the tune of an inaudible soundtrack he imagined being curated by Dean Martin or Sinatra or some other romantic crooner capitalizing on Italian culture.

Further along he saw the harbor, empty at the moment but prepared for many a vessel to moor. Though he was accustomed to life near the water, he was ashamedly naïve to the customs of sailing and fishing or any other nautical endeavors one may partake in. It wasn't due to lack of comprehension, nor to absence of opportunity, that he'd failed to acquire such a skill set, but was, in fact, the result of intentional ignorance. His father had died in a harbor. His head forcibly held under the water until he'd drowned. At least, that's what the authorities had told his mother. A mugging perhaps. And when his father had put up a fight...

Jack lowered his camera and set it aside.

Death had been a common presence in his life.

Perhaps it was a common presence in most people's lives. Should one be fortunate enough to avoid such dark trespasses for any surmountable length of time, it would be quite a feat. Yet he was not one of those lucky few. His history was one of loss. And that was the way of things. No one knows when their time will come. No one knows what ailment will end them, be it a heart attack, or car crash or even drowning.

So what can one do?

Jack clasped his palms around the back of his neck, massaging the muscles that stretched up around his skull. Thinking back to his time in New Jersey, the job he'd done for Congressman Baylor, he imagined himself there. He'd settled into the armchair and twisted open the blinds to reveal the dreary haze between his hotel room window and the restaurant balcony patio across the street. Raising his camera with the mounted telephoto lens, he got a clear view of the well-dressed gentleman — Congressman Jennings — sitting by himself at the corner table. Part of Jack felt like a pretty cold bastard for photographing the private life of an individual — but this particular individual was a politician, and politicians were fair game as far as his morals were concerned.

For the people? What a fucking joke. Any John with a brain knew, as well as any trick with the same, that politicians were out for one person and one person only. You elect people as a popularity contest. Which one of these pricks would we like to see get richer?

Every other week on a Tuesday, Floyd Jennings would visit the same restaurant, sit at the same table and have lunch with a woman — sometimes the same woman, sometimes a different woman, but all of them women who worked for the same pimp — who would then accompany him upstairs to a rented hotel room where they'd fuck.

That particular Tuesday would be the last time that Jack needed to observe that series of events transpiring, because that particular Tuesday, Congressman Floyd Jennings — as Jack knew he'd eventually do — forgot to pull the blinds.

Jennings was one of those men who Jack imagined got where he did in part due to his roguishly charming looks, like JFK or Robert Redford. An all-American man with perfectly curated hair and a movie star smile.

Jack took several photos as the escort adorned herself with the gleaming strap-on. Jennings bent over the edge of the bed, presenting his fuzzy ass in the air. He nodded to the escort, indicating he was ready. She penetrated him. The camera snapped a shot of the man's face contorting.

Jack resurfaced in the present.

He turned to the bed, ready to tuck his camera into his suitcase, when a knock at the door startled him. Surely it was just a member of the staff. Room service. But the recent events made him wish he had a gun with him, same as he carried back home. He'd never had to use it, of course, never had to draw it at all. He'd take it to the range now and then for target practice, but that was the extent of its use. Still, it gave him a sense of security, one he no longer had there in Sicily. One he desperately needed.

He opened the door a crack, seeing the resort manager who had greeted him upon his arrival, waiting with a plastered on smile.

"Yes?" Jack asked.

"So sorry to interrupt, Mr Ivy. I've come to see if there's anything I can help you with. I'm Aldo, the resort manager."

"Yes, I remember."

"Good, yes. It's just, with the unfortunate events as of late, I'm making a point to personally speak with each of our esteemed guests to ensure that their stay is still..."

Jack raised his brow, interested in what word Aldo may choose.

As if Jack's expression helped him realize how absurd the words sounded as he said them, Aldo sighed. "We're all very upset. Devastated really. But I assure you, the police will find the man responsible. There's nothing to worry about."

"Nothing to worry about?"

"Nothing to worry about," Aldo repeated.

"Except for the killer on the loose."

Aldo opened his mouth to say more, but thought better of it. He paused before taking a step back, giving an awkward sort of bow. "If there's anything we can do—"

Jack nodded with a half smile. "But I'm afraid there's not, is there?" And he closed the door.

Luca was behind the bar pouring a glass of white wine for a guest when Jack sat down to order up an afternoon cocktail. Luca's face was flush, his tie loose, and Jack could tell by the man's red eyes that he'd recently been crying, or drinking, or both. Jack checked his watch, seeing it was just past 2pm. He didn't need to ask the bartender what was ailing him. It was all too obvious. The attack of a resort employee, who Luca would have certainly known, was harrowing news to walk into. Jack imagined his shift had started only a few hours ago, so the news was fresh as a wound could be.

"Hi there, Jack," Luca said, feigning an energetic greeting.

"Luca," Jack said with a nod, smelling the scotch on his breath.

"Americano, right?"

Jack scanned the backbar. "Actually, something's put me in the mood for whisky. A J&B on the rocks this time, please."

The slightest grin escaped from beneath the facade plastered across

Luca's face. "Good choice." He poured the drink and set it down in front of Jack.

"Grazie," Jack said, attempting an Italian accent.

"The kitchen's closed at the moment, but they've got the big grills going out on the terrace if you're hungry."

Jack couldn't help but look over at the alley entrance to the kitchen. The police had put yellow barrier tape up for good measure.

"I'm all right at the moment."

Luca returned the bottle of scotch to the backbar. "You picked one hell of a week to visit this place."

"I was very sorry to hear about your co-worker. Have you heard how she's doing?"

"One of my friends here called me at home first thing this morning and let me know what had happened, so I went by the hospital and saw her on my way into work. She's holding up, stab wound in the shoulder and a bit of lingering hypothermia from being locked in the cooler all night."

"*Stabbed?*" Jack asked. "Did she identify the man?"

"Couldn't see his face." Luca leaned back against the ice bin. "I'd seen her just before it all happened. I was probably five minutes down the road while she was fighting for her life."

"God, I'm sorry, Luca."

"Management offered a few days off if any of us wanted time to process it all."

"Might be a good idea," Jack said.

"Probably. But *someone* needs to keep their ear to the ground, find out what the hell's going on. May as well be me."

"Isn't that what the police are for?" Jack asked, knowing full well his own negative experiences with law enforcement, but trying to remain positive for Luca's sake.

"The police?" Luca chuckled. "Too many times I've seen their true selves come out after a few drinks. They're all hateful bullies who joined the biggest gang they could find to finance their violent urges. I don't know how it is in America, but in my experience, I've never met an officer I could trust. The mafia do a better job policing than the actual cops."

Luca motioned toward Jack's forgotten glass of scotch.

Jack obliged.

"You know, I think these two attacks are related," Luca said. "In fact, I'm convinced of it."

Jack hesitated before spewing out his thoughts. "If it were the same man, and Elio Gaeta didn't kill his wife, then how the hell did someone get into their room and murder her without him noticing? A person doesn't just sleep through something like that."

"They might if they were dead drunk. How many more drinks did he have after I left?" Luca asked.

Jack ruminated on it. Elio had been drunk. But had he been *that* drunk? Drunk enough not to hear his wife slashed apart a few feet away? Or maybe he was drugged, Jack considered. Something sprinkled in his drink? Jack kept the thought to himself, not wanting it to sound like he was insinuating the bartender had done anything malicious.

"He looked pretty sloshed. Still coherent though."

Luca rested on his elbows, folding his hands in front of his face. "Illaria—that's her name, Illaria—she said that whoever attacked her had some sort of military dagger. Something old. Antique maybe, but she couldn't quite place it. When I was leaving, I overheard some of the officers at the hospital talking about it too. Surprise, surprise, they let a few details slip."

Jack leaned in closer as Luca's voice softened.

"Apparently, the same type of knife was found in Vittoria Gaeta's back."

Jack winced at the thought.

"They think it may have been a Blackshirt's dagger."

"Blackshirt's dagger?" Jack asked.

"Blackshirts were Italian fascists. When Mussolini was ousted as Prime Minister and Italy switched sides during the war to join the allied forces, the Nazis rescued old Il Duce. Hitler made him Prime Minister of the RSI, allowing Mussolini to have his own personal militia, the so-called Brigate Nere — Black Brigades — made up of Italian fascists. Their purpose was simple: to stamp out partisans and help Nazis massacre Italian civilians."

"Christ," Jack said, taking another drink.

"Now, it's no secret that Vittoria Gaeta's father, Carlo Rossini, was a member of the Black Brigades. It was a hot topic for all the trash rags when her career blew up. She even went on record shortly after denouncing her father's actions during the war, and fascism as a whole."

Another guest interrupted their conversation to order a drink. Luca prepared it, then returned and continued in an even lower voice.

"Illaria..." Luca had to pause a moment to keep himself composed. Jack considered reaching across the bar to put a hand on the bartender's shoulder to comfort him. Luca cleared his throat and continued his story. "Illaria and I are close. Close enough for her to share personal things here and there. She, too, had a father in the Black Brigade. He killed himself after the war, supposedly stricken with guilt over the atrocities he had committed."

"Both victims were daughters of fascists. You think that's why they were targeted?" Jack asked.

"Maybe. A Blackshirt's dagger left at the crime scene? Seems telling, doesn't it? Like the killer is sending a message?"

"Why here at Terme del Paradiso? There must be millions of Italians whose families were involved with that regime."

Luca glanced around the lounge as if determining whether it was safe to verbalize what he was about to say next. "Illaria wasn't the only co-worker who shared personal details with me. Sometimes after their shifts, staff members will change out of uniform and have a drink or two at the bar. When people drink, they talk. One of those talkers was someone they only recently hired. A guy named Marco."

Marco. That was the name of the attendant Jack had spoken to earlier that morning. The one that had such unsettling things to say regarding the cook's attack. Was this the same man?

"Turns out Marco lost both his wife and daughter to the Black Brigade during the war," Luca said. "They were slaughtered in the village of Sant'Anna di Stazzema, along with nearly six hundred other innocent Italian men, women, and children."

Jack took another sip of his scotch. "You're saying—"

"I'm saying he has a motive. That's all."

"Which is?"

Luca's brow raised as he said, "Sins of the father."

Chapter 12
Head Above Water

Outside the town of Randazzo, near the northern foot of Mount Etna, a homestead crippled by years of neglect sat forgotten in a sea of scorched soil and dead vegetation. As the taxi retreated, leaving a tail of dust in its wake, Silvia approached the front door with hesitation. She dried her sweaty hands on her dress, then took a deep breath and rapped upon the door.

Inside, she heard something fall and roll across the floor, and a gravely voice muttered obscenities. Through the gaps in the wooden slat door, she could see someone moving about, drifting in and out of sight. Then she heard the unmistakable metallic snap of a break-action shotgun. She'd spent many hours on the clay grounds of her late-husband's family palazzo, watching him practice his aim with the double-barrel his grandfather had handed down. Repeatedly, he would crack open the barrel to reload, tossing the smoking shells aside for the servants to collect. It had ingrained the sound in her mind.

"Father, it's me!" Silvia shouted through the door, stepping aside in case the old man was too quick on the draw.

"Silvia?" the gravely voice called. The rickety door moaned open on rusted hinges and a hunched man with leathery, sun-scarred skin crept out. He let the shotgun hang at his side, the weight of it pulling him toward the ground. Squinting in the sunlight, his brittle frame peered around the door and sized his daughter up. He chewed his tongue and ran his hand along his scalp, brushing back the wispy strands of white hair from his cloudy brown eyes.

"It's me," she repeated.

"Of course it is. Yes, of course." He nodded and waved for her to follow him inside. As the door closed behind her, blocking out the sunlight — save for a few beams that sliced in through the gaps in the door — Silvia's eyes adjusted to the murkiness of the interior. An eternal haze of dust seemed to hang in the air, lingering over the sparse, decrepit furniture and filth covered clutter in the corners. She thought it looked like the set of a Western film — one of those 19th century American farmsteads where a retired outlaw was living out his final days. The only thing that seemed out of place was the framed painting of Benito Mussolini above the fireplace. It was immaculately clean, as though main-taining its appearance had become her father's sole priority.

Silvia's father set the shotgun down on the table, which she assumed he ate all his meals at alone, then collapsed into his armchair the way old folks do when the muscles in their legs have abandoned them.

"I'm glad you came," he said, gesturing toward the ramshackle sofa. "I've missed your face. But that's what photographs are for, I suppose."

She took a seat, keeping to the very edge of the dirty cushion. "And how have you been?"

"Still here. Still surviving."

Silvia thought it was the perfect way to describe how her father was living. *Surviving.* The house was little more than a rickety structure to keep him dry in the rain, and she doubted whether it even accomplished that.

"No thanks to the people in charge, of course," he added.

"Did you invite me here to talk politics?"

Her father laughed. "You know why I invited you here, Silvia."

She paused before answering. "Because you're dying."

A smile forced its way into existence, morphing the wrinkled skin of the old man's face. "I've been dying for years. That's nothing new."

"Why then? To apologize?"

"*Apologize?* For what?"

"For deserting me."

"You play the game of life alone, child. We all have our responsibilities, and we're both too old now for me to be parenting you. Asking me to stomach those *partisans* and their spoiled son was far too great a request. I don't know how you did it all those years, living with him and his traitorous, activist family." He shook his head as if he could wipe the image from his mind. "But at least you have their money now. So, something good came from it. No?"

Silvia kept her composure. "Answer my question. Why now?"

"Because the bastard is dead. Because you're mine again. And because sometimes photographs just *aren't* enough."

"And sometimes they're everything. In fact, there's one I'd like to have, if you've still got it around. The one Mom used to keep on her nightstand."

Her father cocked his head, surprised by the request. "The one your mother—" Standing, he waded across the room and rummaged through the rickety bookshelf, sifting through tattered tomes and discarded junk.

"She kept it in a bronze fame," Silvia added.

"I know," he said, still searching. "I know the one."

He turned back to face her, a yellowed black-and-white photograph in his hands. He stared at it for a moment before walking back and handing it to Silvia. She looked at the worn print of the four men in black military uniforms standing shoulder to shoulder, all of them wearing the same stoic face young men make to appear tough.

"She loved that photo. And she loved what it stood for. I was about your age there. Idealistic. Full of hope. Knowing Il Duce would lead us to a better life." He looked up at the painting of Mussolini above the fireplace. "One that never came to be thanks to all those traitors... like your husband's parents."

Silvia knew that even after all these years, there were still fascists in

Italy who viewed Mussolini with sympathy, seeing him as the man who lifted the country out of the Great Depression and into the modern age. They saw him as a savior, unjustly vilified.

"You want some tea? I think I might have some in the cupboard," her father said.

"Tea would be nice."

He ambled into the kitchen area, sifting between jars of pickled vegetables until he found a container of loose leaf tea. As he lit the stove to boil a kettle, the sound of approaching tires on the dirt road outside drove him back to his shotgun. Scooping it up, he went to the shuttered window and peered out through the tiny gaps.

"What is it?" Silvia asked.

Her father didn't answer. She could hear the unexpected vehicle come to a halt. The slam of car doors preceded steps on the stoop, and an aggressive knock at the door followed.

"Frezza," a voice from beyond the door called.

Silvia stood, and her father gestured for her to stay back.

Another knock at the door. Her father pulled it open, revealing two men in dark suits and hats. They stared at her father and the shotgun in his hand, as though it had deeply offended them, and without a word, he quickly placed it back on the table. Then the men entered, both of them dismissing her father, their eyes settling on Silvia.

"You have company," the first man said. He was tall, with jet black hair and a thin mustache perfectly shaped above his lip. "I didn't know the whores made house calls this far out of town."

"Excuse me?" Silvia said, taking an aggressive step forward.

Her father stepped between them. "My daughter," he said. "Silvia."

"*Daughter?*" The mustachioed man waved for her father to move aside, then looked Silvia up and down. He pointed at her with his index finger and made a swirling motion. "Spin around for me."

"I most certainly will not."

The mustachioed man looked over at Silvia's father, who then said, "He just wants to see your dress, Silvia."

She glared at her father, his cowardice on full display. These men in the expensive suits, whoever they were, had reduced her war veteran father to a trembling mess.

"He can see my dress just fine."

"Spin," the man repeated.

The second man pulled a pack of cigarettes and a lighter from his breast pocket and lit up. Taking a long drag, he prominently displayed the gold ring on his pinky finger. Silvia recognized it immediately. Hell, all of Sicily knew it. What had her father gotten himself mixed up in?

"Silvia," her father urged in a quiet, pleading tone.

Silvia took a deep breath before doing a lazy pirouette. The mustachioed man laughed and clapped condescendingly.

"Bravo."

Clenching her jaw, Silvia held back the words boiling in her head.

"Now, turn and face the wall while we speak with your father," the man instructed. "I like the view better from that side."

"Go fuck yourself." She could hardly believe she'd said it out loud. The two mafiosos leered at her, then the one with the ring turned to her father, cocking his head as if waiting for him to respond.

Silvia's father, his hands shaking like an alcoholic going through withdrawals, converged on her. He hesitated only a moment before striking her across the cheek with the back of his hand. Silvia stumbled, catching herself on the armchair, knocking over a stack of photographs in the process.

The mustachioed man laughed again, patting her father on the back. "Very good, Frezza. A daughter must know her place, yes?"

Silvia's fingers curled, digging into the side of the leather chair. All three men watched her, awaiting her response. She could see the shame in her father's eyes as he stared at her. Whether it was for laying his hands on her, or for failing to teach her how to hold her tongue, she couldn't be sure.

"Last chance," the mustachioed man said. "Face the wall while we conduct our business with your father."

A single tear escaped from Silvia's eye, and she slowly turned away, her fingers still gouging her father's chair. She listened as the men chastised her father, threatening not to give him what they came to deliver because of his daughter's petulance. He begged them to reconsider, whining that he desperately needed the money he was owed. Silvia could tell by the sound of their voices that they were enjoying the agony they were putting him through, reveling in every stutter, every plead. The mustachioed man chuckled and Silvia glanced over her shoulder, seeing him pull an envelope from his jacket and toss it flippantly onto the table.

Sensing her gaze, he turned and saw her peeking. Silvia immediately looked away, knowing she'd been caught. Making *tisk-tisk* clicks with his tongue, he strolled over, pressing himself against her backside. His head extended over her shoulder so that their profiles aligned and he said, "So curious. You're like a little cat, unable to control her impulses, aren't you?"

His hand slid down her dress, fingers hooking around the bottom, slowly raising it up her hips. Silvia shuttered, pinned against the chair, her father standing idly by as the man groped her in front of him. She felt his fingers worm through her hair, then suddenly they constricted and her head was yanked back, exposing her neck. The man's lips pressed against her throat as he whispered, "Should I teach you how to behave?"

Then he shoved her away, and she landed hard on the debris-riddled floor. The man laughed and joined his partner in the doorway.

"Wait," Silvia's father said. "Is there more work?"

Silvia looked up at him from the floor, his soul laid bare by the desperation on his face. His hand was extended out toward the men, like a starving child begging for charity.

"We know where to find you if you're needed, Frezza," the man with the ring said. Then they left, and as the sound of their car faded away, Silvia's father watched from the window.

She mourned what had become of him. A once proud soldier, now reduced to a lowly peasant who'd sell out his own daughter to keep his head above water. For a long while, she waited for him to say something, anything, but he dared not even look her way. The photograph he had handed her of his younger self and his brothers-in-arms lay on the floor, one of many memories of a man who no longer existed. She picked it up, and without another word, left the home of the man who had once been Silvano Frezza.

Chapter 13
Marco & The Maid

Beneath the shade of a cabana, Jack laid atop a lounge chair in his swim shorts and linen shirt, his eye line hidden behind a pair of rectangular framed sunglasses from a designer he'd never heard of. Though the neon blue pool was graced by a plethora of bikini-clad women, his sights zeroed in on the blue-eyed resort attendant standing at attention beside the towel rack. Marco (as the man's name tag stated) was involved in all of this madness somehow, and whether he was the deadly killer Luca had insinuated him to be, he had rubbed Jack the wrong way with his creepy statements in the lobby. Someone needed to keep their ear to the ground, as Luca had said, and Jack knew this Marco character was someone worth listening out for.

It was a far cry from his normal stakeouts in Jersey: sitting in some sweaty van, staring through the viewfinder of his camera at his target across the way, listening to the mundane voice of a radio DJ drown out the sound of city traffic. Here, in Sicily, he couldn't help but feel a bit like James Bond off on one of his jet-setting adventures, indulging in the life of luxury while casually searching for his next lead to point him to the villain's lair. The exotic locale, beautiful women, and suspicious Europeans, it was all here. And the death. He couldn't forget about the death. But unlike those Bond films, the horror of it lingered, permeating his every thought, soaking into his brain, unable to be wrung out.

A handsome couple strolled into view, searching for the perfect spot to nestle in, selecting a cabana right beside Jack. Marco immediately hustled over to them with a pair of bone white towels, placing them perfectly on the table. Without acknowledging him, they continued their conversation, and he retreated to his station.

"Beautiful day."

Jack realized the husband was addressing to him. He must have assumed Jack was looking at them while he was watching Marco deliver the towels.

"Beautiful day," Jack echoed.

"You're American," the husband said. "Us too. Where're you from?"

Jack wasn't there for conversation. "New Jersey. You?"

"California," the wife answered. "But Sicily is our home away from home. At least it's going to be after this trip. It's our first time here."

"Mine too," Jack said.

"We're traveling all across Italy. This is our last stop. We already saw Rome, Florence—"

"And Naples," the husband interrupted.

"God, Naples." the wife sighed with delight, laying back in her lounge chair. "Have you been?"

"I haven't," Jack said.

"You absolutely must."

Jack nodded and smiled, trying to keep one eye on Marco while simultaneously feigning interest in engaging with the couple. "I'll add it to the list."

"It's where pizza was invented. Did you know that?"

"In Naples? Can't say I did."

She rolled onto her side to face Jack, raising her sunglasses to rest atop her head. "Are you here with your wife?"

"No, not married."

"Girlfriend?" she asked. The flirtation in her question wasn't hidden, and yet her husband was unbothered. In fact, Jack sensed he was just as interested in the answer to the question as she was.

Jack laughed to cover his discomfort. "Uh, no. I'm here alone."

The husband placed his hand on his wife's thigh, and she smiled over her shoulder at him. "I'm gonna grab us some drinks," he said, then looked at Jack. "Anything for you, friend?"

"I'm all set, but thank you."

The husband gave his wife a slap on the ass as he stood, and she responded with an excited yelp. Jack raised his eyebrows, surprised by the public display. "Be right back," the husband said, departing for the shaded poolside bar.

"You sure you don't want a drink? Our treat," the wife coaxed.

"The day's long. I need to pace myself."

"You don't *need* to do anything. That's the best part of being on vacation," she said.

But that wasn't true. Not for Jack. He had a job to do, even if he wasn't being paid for it.

Like a sentry guarding the entrance to some medieval castle, Marco stood beside the rack of beach towels, his gaze ever watchful for guests in need. Jack wasn't sure what he expected to see. An old dagger tucked behind the man's back? It's not as if Marco was going to slash one of the women apart right there in broad daylight with all these witnesses. It'd be at night, just like the last two had.

Of course. Why hadn't Jack considered it before? It was so simple. He needed to get a hold of the resort's staff schedule. That way, he'd know where and when Marco would be on duty. Maybe he could tail him as soon as he clocked out, see where he goes. Jack figured he could find a schedule in the manager's office, or maybe a staff break room. Hell, maybe Luca could just hand him a copy.

"You gonna take a dip?" The wife motioned toward the pool.

"Maybe in a bit," he said, glancing at the beautiful women wading about as though they were in the midst of a modeling gig.

"It's so ridiculous, isn't it? A pool sitting only a hundred feet from the ocean, all of us spending our time in a man-made body of water instead of that giant, gorgeous natural one."

"I can think of another body I wouldn't mind being inside of," the husband said as he sat back down with a pair of colorful cocktails.

"Stop it! Oh, my god!" The wife slapped him on the leg.

They both laughed, and the husband kissed her neck. She gazed over at Jack as her husband's lips continued to taste her.

Jack looked away. "You know, I think I do want a drink after all," he said.

"Oh, well, let me run back over and grab you one," the husband said.

"No, no." Jack was already on his feet. "Thank you, but I can manage."

"We'll be right here," the wife called after Jack as he strolled toward the poolside bar.

He wasn't about to add a ménage à trois to his agenda for the day. Pretending not to hear her, he turned his back to the couple as he bellied up to the counter. He ordered a drink, and as he sat beneath the shade of the palm leaf the awning, he monitored his target.

A resort maid with a fresh stack of folded towels approached Marco and the two of them conversed, the expressions on both their faces oddly dour. When she placed the towels on the rack and turned to leave, Marco's hand clamped aggressively around her wrist and held her in place.

Jack instinctively stood as though he might run over and pry the man's grip loose.

Marco leaned in close to the maid, whispering something in her ear, then she shook herself free and immediately left the area with haste. Jack looked around to see if anyone else at the pool had witnessed the altercation, but the guests and staff alike were oblivious. Leaving his untouched cocktail on the bar top, he quickly, but casually, followed the maid.

Down the wide, stone steps, which bled into a walkway below a terrace overlooking the water, Jack traced her path, keeping a safe distance so as not to alarm her. He'd need to get her isolated, somewhere he could question her, free of suspicious eyes. Maybe he could pull her aside, into a closet, or an office...

Right. That wouldn't look dubious at all, would it?

Unscrupulous Foreigner Forces Resort Maid Into Closet!

Inspector Righetti would love that headline. A single phone call from a random staff member and Jack would be down at the police station for questioning, all while Marco continued to walk free.

The maid stepped inside through a staff door, and Jack kept his line of sight through the window. A full team of service staff shared the space, rows of washing machines and dryers lining the wall. The maid stood facing the corner, hands perched on her hips, head low. Jack imagined she was decompressing from whatever the conversation with Marco had entailed. One of the attendants said something to her in Italian, motioning to a maid's trolley. She nodded and loaded it up with clean towels before exiting the laundry room.

Jack pretended to be admiring the scenery when she passed by, then followed as she entered the lobby through a side entrance, watching as she made her way to the elevator and ascended to the third floor. This was his opportunity.

He called the elevator back down to the lobby, then took it up to her level, spotting the maid as she handed a stack of towels to the guest in room 402. As soon as the door closed, and Jack and the maid were alone in the hall, he waved and called, "Excuse me."

The maid turned to him. "How can I help, sir?" Then her face darkened, as though she recognized him as some long forgotten villain.

"I was hoping you could help me with something."

"Of course, sir," she said, the irritated tone in her voice betraying the mandatory hospitality verbiage.

"Right over here, in my room." Jack gestured for her to accompany him as he strolled down the hall.

"I've been instructed to deliver these towels at the moment, sir. I can send someone else to see to your needs if you just tell me what it is we can assist with."

"It'll only take a moment of your time. I'm in a bit of a hurry," Jack said, still walking toward his room.

"What room number are you in? I can send someone over shortly." She was still standing beside room 402.

"No, no. Just come help me. I can't wait for that." The distance between them was growing, and Jack was getting louder, the volume putting the pressure on the maid to comply for fear of being heard arguing with a guest.

"Sir—"

"Right over here, please. I can't be kept waiting now."

Jack could see the reluctance in her steps as she finally began walking toward him. He opened the door to his room and called out again, "Is this what they call hospitality at Terme del Paradiso? I haven't got all day." The words felt so cruel coming out of his mouth, but he knew the threat of reprimand by the resort manager was the only card he had to play in order to get her into his room.

The maid picked up her pace, leaving the trolley unattended in the hall. She hesitated once more before crossing the threshold into Jack's room, then once inside she asked, "What is it I can be of assistance with, sir?"

As Jack closed the door, he noticed the sound of the latch caused the maid to shudder. He sighed, hating the fear he was causing to billow up inside her.

"I'm Jack," he said, holding out his hand.

She kept her arms at her side and repeated, "What is it I can be of assistance with, sir?" She was young, her hair pulled back in a tight bun, and as her eyes dared to raise from the floor and look at him, Jack finally realized where the trepidation was stemming from.

He'd seen her before. And she had seen him... two nights prior in the elevator with Vittoria. She had been there when the doors opened, Vittoria's hand down Jack's pants. She knew Jack had been with her the night of the murder. No wonder she seemed so afraid.

"I didn't kill her," he blurted out.

"I don't know what you're talking about." Her eyes darted away.

"I remember you from that night. I know you saw us together, as did many others, but I didn't kill Vittoria Gaeta."

"You don't have to convince me, sir. If that's why you brought me in here—"

"I saw you at the pool with that attendant. Marco. I think he may know something about the attacks."

"I don't know what anyone knows other than myself. And I know nothing."

"No? So what is it the two of you were talking about? Seemed like a rather heated discussion."

"It was nothing. Now if there isn't anything—"

"What's your name?" Jack asked.

"What does that—"

"What's your name?"

She took a deep breath and answered, "Monica."

"Listen, Monica. I know you know something. Something more than you're letting on. All I want to do is help put an end to all this."

Tears welled up in her eyes. "I can't. I don't want to die."

"*Die?* Why would you die?" Jack waited for a response. "Why would you die, Monica?"

"I saw someone. Last night, in the basement. My supervisor sent me down there to grab a box of labels. There's usually never anyone down there, especially that late at night, so near the end of my shift. We just use the space for storage, mostly. But someone was standing in front of the furnace. They had it open, and they were throwing things inside. Clothes. A raincoat. A hat."

"Who was it?" The urgency in Jack's voice swelled.

"I don't know. There isn't much light down there other than the fire from the furnace, and when I saw them..." She paused, and Jack could see her revisiting the memory in her mind. "They didn't have a face."

"What do you mean, they didn't have a face?"

"It was a mask. It must have been a mask." She nodded, reassuring herself. "And this morning when I heard about that cook, I started thinking about the timeframe, and... I — I think it could have been the person who attacked her."

"They were destroying evidence," Jack said.

"They saw me. And now I'm afraid they'll come after me next if I say anything to the police. Better to keep my mouth shut. We all know what happens to witnesses who speak up."

"And Marco? You think he may be the killer? The one you saw at the furnace?"

"I can't say anymore." Monica spun and reached for the doorknob, but Jack caught her by the arm — the same arm he'd seen Marco grab earlier at the pool. She looked up at him with terror, as though she expected him to slap her across the face.

"Has he threatened you? Is that it?"

"Let me go!" She tugged her arm free, and shoved Jack away, then flung the door open and escaped into the hall.

Jack stepped out behind her and froze when he saw Giancarlo — the concierge — standing a few feet away from the door. Giancarlo watched Monica storm away, her face red and wet with tears. Then he turned to Jack in the doorway.

The two men stared blankly at one another, Jack sure that this was the moment he'd sealed his fate. He knew the concierge's next move would be to phone the police, accusing him of whatever imaginary scenario he'd dreamt up after seeing a young woman flee his room in tears.

A grin spread across Giancarlo's face. He shrugged and said, "Women. I'm more than happy to get you proper company, sir... if that's what you're looking for."

Jack couldn't believe what he was hearing. Proper company? Was this weaselly little man moonlighting as the resort's pimp? Was a terrified, crying employee commonplace here?

"No. Thank you. I'll be just fine." He could hardly get the words out.

"Of course you will. Handsome man like you? Monica is no slouch, but I hear you've been having plenty of fun with all the best looking ladies here."

Jack hated knowing his escapades were such common knowledge. The gossipy staff was no doubt reveling in all the rumors surrounding the attacks.

Giancarlo tipped his head and waited at attention until Jack finally closed the door, sealing himself away inside his room.

Chapter 14
The Massage

Night breathed across Sicily as Silvia arrived back at Terme del Paradiso. The reality of her father's current life weighed heavily on her mind, and even after stopping at the Corso Umberto in Taormina to wander about the shops, her head was no clearer than it had been the moment she left her father's homestead.

While the existence of the mafia was no secret to anyone in Italy, the revelation that her father, a man whom she had grown up idolizing, had reduced himself to an errand boy for them pained her deeply. The sight of the great Silvano Frezza cowering to criminals inside his own home, so afraid that he couldn't even stand up for his own daughter, was heartbreaking. This was a man who'd fought in the war, battled the enemy with every sinew of his being. How had her hero fallen so far?

But as much as she wanted there to be some big mystery to it all, the answer could not have been more simple. Money. It was always money. He had no work, none but whatever illicit opportunities the mafia offered him, and therein lied the harsh reality of why he must have wanted to reconnect with Silvia after all these years. The inheritance that she'd received from her late husband could turn her father's life around. It could pull him up out of the squalor he'd been struggling to survive in.

But perhaps he'd been too proud to ask for such a favor from his daughter. Perhaps it gnawed at some inner shred of self-respect still lingering deep inside him. Would it really be any more of an offense than stooping to criminal activities in service of the mafia?

For him?

Of course it would.

Silvia knew her father could never ask outright. Relying on a woman for help was an embarrassment. Her father was no exception when it came to the way men viewed women. The way things are and the way things ought to be are always so far apart.

As she went to her room, she thought about visiting the lounge for a drink to relax, but she didn't want to converse with anyone, not even Jack. If he saw she was back, he'd want to catch up, and Silvia's day had already been over-saturated with what *men* wanted.

Calling down to reception, she asked that they make a massage appointment for her, and though the hour was late, they accommodated, agreeing to keep the masseuse on duty for a while longer.

She set the old photograph of her father and the other three soldiers on the bedside table. The youthful face of her father stared up at her, his slick, dark uniform so contrasting with the stained and tattered clothing she'd seen him in only hours earlier. She flipped the photograph over to cast away the past, and the hand-written inscription on the back came into view.

Frezza, Conti, Rossini & Cairo — 1943

She popped open her clamshell pillbox and sifted through her little helpers. There were the white ones that put her right to sleep, the yellows that provided a pick-me-up, and the powder blues that gave her mind room to wander. She chose the latter and swallowed it with a glass of water, then took the elevator back down to the main floor where she checked in at the spa desk.

The attendant, a handsome man, trim with chiseled features, led her to the changing rooms, provided Silvia with a plush robe, and waited outside the door while she stripped down. Donning the robe, Silvia's fingers traced the embroidered resort logo on the chest as she looked at herself in the full-length mirror.

Down a hallway lined with private rooms, the attendant led her to the last door on the left. He ushered Silvia inside, and before leaving, informed her the masseuse would be in shortly. "Afterward you are welcome to use the other amenities," he said. "Steam room, sauna, hot and cold showers, vanities. Whatever you like."

Silvia removed her robe and hung it on the back of the door, then slid onto the table and pulled the sheet over her lower half. For a few moments, she was alone with the gentle music, the warmth of the private room cocooning her. When the door opened, she left her head resting on the table, her eyes closed. She felt the masseuse adjust the sheet, lowering it down a few inches further, then a pair of hands soft with warm oil glided across her, slowly priming every inch of her skin. Starting at her neck, they applied pressure; the fingertips rotating around each muscle, honing in like bloodhounds tracking prey. But as the hands forced the tension in her shoulders to release, pressing the knots against the edges of her shoulder blades, vanquishing their once unquestioned rule over her body, Silvia's mind fought its own war.

The faces of the mafiosos refused to leave her, their sour grins and vulgar words like ocean waves receding for a moment, only to return with a violent crash. The man's golden family ring. The other's thin mustache above his grinning mouth. *Spin.*

In her mind, their laughs were the soundtrack to the image of her father striking her across the cheek.

You're like a little cat, unable to control her impulses, aren't you?

Should I teach you how to behave?

The hands of the masseuse and the memory of the mafioso's touch melded, the intended relaxation tainted by the growing concern that she had yet to see the face of the man massaging her. Were they the same person? Had the mafiosos followed her back to the resort and snuck into the spa?

No. She knew it couldn't be them. She was being ridiculous. Why would they go through all that trouble just to—

Teach her how to behave?

The hands continued to knead her skin, and the visions of the mafiosos morphed into Elio Gaeta, dressed in his black raincoat and hat just as he had been when she first saw him after arriving at the resort. And then the violence arrived, saturating her thoughts, the delirium of Vittoria being stabbed, the knife penetrating her naked body, over and over. So much blood.

But no screams of pain emanated from Vittoria's mouth. Instead, she seemed to moan with pleasure. The knife had vanished, replaced by—

Her little blue pill was in full effect. Silvia's mind was certainly wandering now. The arousing mental image engulfed her, and the sound of Vittoria's moans drowned out the gentle music.

Then a voice cut through the fantasy.

"Turn over for me." It was the masseuse. Or at least Silvia thought it was. Maybe that had been in her head as well? She felt the sheet lift off her legs and she slowly rolled over onto her back. As she opened her eyes, the face of the masseuse was obscured by the union of her blurred vision and the candlelight.

His hands gently grabbed her shoulders, and using his thumbs, he began massaging below her clavicle. Silvia closed her eyes, her mind drifting back to the vision of Vittoria, and the masseuse's hands became hers. She straddled atop Silvia on the massage table; her thumbs applying pressure. A flash of light exploded across the dim room, and in a second, it was gone. Then another, bright as sunlight, radiated brilliantly, this time accompanied by the snap of a camera shutter. Vittoria posed naked atop Silvia, modeling for some unseen phantom.

"That's it," the invisible photographer said. "Just like that."

Another snap of the shutter.

"Now put your hands on her breasts."

There was something familiar about his voice, but Silvia couldn't focus as Vittoria's hands slithered down her body.

Snap. Snap. Snap. The photographer captured the sensual display. Vittoria leaned down, her lips melting into Silvia's.

"Good. Goooood," the photographer whispered.

Why do I know that voice?

Vittoria's fingers entered her, and Silvia gasped.

Snap. Snap. Snap.

"Now..." the photographer said. "For the finale."

And Silvia gasped as she finally placed the voice. She looked across the room, her eyes searching the shadows, finding the man behind the camera.

Jack.

He stood there watching; the camera obscuring half his face, a smile peeking out from below the lens. With his index finger hovering above the shutter button, he said, "Kill her."

Silvia looked up to see Vittoria, her arms raised above her head, holding something that would only be revealed once the camera flash went off. The light glinted off the blade of the dagger, and Vittoria brought it straight down into Silvia's chest.

The sound of a door slamming shut disintegrated everything in the room. Vittoria, Jack, the knife, even the room itself vanished. Silvia sat up, no longer on the massage table. She was back in her hotel room, lying in bed, the corner lamp softly illuminating reality.

Her breathing was rapid, nearing hyperventilation. She touched her bare chest, her fingers tracing the spot the dagger had entered her.

But it hadn't entered her. There was no wound. No blood. She slid out of bed, creeping across the room to ensure she was truly alone. The bathroom door was slightly ajar. Pressing gently, she widened the gap, part of her expecting to see some intruder waiting for her. But there was no one there, no one preparing to attack.

It had all been the effects of the powder blue pill, she thought. *Nothing more.*

It was a hell of a drug, after all. When her mind needed a break from the world, it was the quickest way to do it. A psychedelic experience, they called it.

The worst part was always the aftermath, not knowing where the hallucinations began and ended. Had she even gone down to the spa at all? If so, how had she gotten back to her room? A staff member, perhaps?

Maybe that would explain the sound of the door slamming. It could have been them leaving the room after helping her into bed.

But maybe she *hadn't* gone down to the spa. Maybe she'd taken the pill, and the trip had begun before she made it out of the room. It could have all happened in her head. The conversation with the receptionist, the massage, all of it. Maybe she had simply been lying there in bed the whole time as her mind flitted about the ether.

But if that was the case, then no one would have had to help her back. So who had slammed the door? And even more worrisome: what had they been doing in her room?

Chapter 15
The Cabana Crowd

Jack checked his watch.

11pm.

He discarded the idea of stealing the staff schedule after weighing the consequences of anyone seeing him. How would he explain that one to the Inspector? He knew what it would look like. A roadmap to a killing spree. He couldn't risk it.

If Monica was working the same schedule as she had the day before, then, by his estimate, it was nearing the end of her shift. She had said she'd seen someone throwing clothes into the furnace just before she left for the night, placing the occurrence right around 11:30pm. According to her, there was usually no one down in the basement this late at night, so, if he wanted to look for evidence of Monica's story, now would be the time to do so.

He vacated his seat in the empty lobby and attempted to appear as casual as possible before making his move. The room at the end of the hallway would take him where he wanted to go, and with no lock on the door, he was able to slip through without being noticed.

A concrete staircase led down to the dark room, his shoes brushing against each step as he descended. An orange glow emanated from the far end — the furnace. Its iron door, like a medieval knight's armored visor, let warmth escape through the slits, luring Jack closer with the promise of comfort. Although he felt rather certain he was alone, he kept a watchful eye on the shadows.

Unsure of what he expected to find, knowing a full twenty-four hours of burning would have certainly disintegrated any remnants of the unwanted clothing, Jack searched the area. Resting against a support beam, a fire poker awaited him. He picked it up, feeling the weight in his hand, then, using the hooked end, pulled down on the furnace grate handle and unlatched the door. The hinges moaned, and the flames snapped outward like captive serpents in a basket.

Squinting in the intense light, Jack observed the edges of the opening, hoping to find some shred of material left behind, perhaps protected by the metal of the door. With the sharp end of the poker, he prodded at the frame, then let the fire heat the metal until it glowed hot. As he removed it, he held it up to his face, watching the heat slowly dissipate until the poker returned to its natural dark appearance.

Jack wondered whether Monica had ever requested a change of shifts. There was no denying the basement was a rather intimidating and unsettling environment, and being down there alone nearing midnight heightened the spookiness. Add that to seeing a strange masked figure burning clothing in the furnace and you had the perfect ingredients for a horror tale. She must have been utterly terrified.

Setting the poker back against the beam, Jack turned his attention to the floor. The dusty concrete was a collage of footprints, most of them smeared and morphing into an unidentifiable mess. There were staff down here on the daily, throwing any manner of articles into the furnace. If Illaria's attacker had been down here and left prints in the dust, there would be no way for Jack to distinguish them.

Feeling there was nothing left to inspect in the basement, Jack made his way back up the staircase, careful not to draw any attention as he slipped back through the doorway. He passed the employee break room, stealing a look at the few staff members enjoying a dose of late night caffeine to help them through the rest of their shift. Some he recognized, yet none were Monica. And none were Marco, who he hadn't seen since the pool. Jack assumed it was likely he'd already finished for the day. The question was whether the man was still lurking around off the clock.

Outside, the cabana bar was in full swing. The men, dressed in their turtleneck sweaters and leisure suits, were a collage of burgundy and shades of patterned brown, while the women in their casual evening dresses formed a sea of peacock blue and bottle green. They drank and laughed, huddled beneath the palm leaf awning. White lights hung overhead, casting an ethereal hue as though they were a group of Olympian gods partying the night away, uninterested and unbothered by the troubles of mere mortals. How much money did it take, Jack wondered, for both a murder and an attempted murder to occur where you're residing and still be so at ease? Did these people think they were untouchable? Invincible?

It had only been two days since Vittoria's death. *One* since Illaria was attacked. Yet there they all stood, as though nothing had happened. And that's exactly what it was, Jack thought. Nothing. At least to the rest of the guests. Just some little scribble in the notepad of life. Terrible, violent things happened every day all around the world. Why should these two events hold any significance to strangers? When you don't know the victim personally, death can mean so little.

But Jack *did* know one of the victims. Even if it was for the briefest of time. Vittoria's death was no footnote in his life's book. She'd become a whole bloody chapter, and Jack was determined to help find a proper ending.

The further he could distance himself from the cabana crowd, the better. He left them behind, walking along the perimeter of the resort until he found himself at the entrance of the gardens. Roses of every shade, like shards of stained glass, filled the hedges. Jack considered smelling one but felt too self-conscious and refrained. Was that something one does in a garden like this? Smell the roses? He'd never seen someone stoop to take a sniff before, imagining how awkward it might look. Then again, he'd never been in a rose garden, so etiquette was complete speculation.

As he strolled in deeper, the hedges seemed to guide him, leading left then right, every row ripe with floral beauty. His next step landed on uneven ground and something slid beneath his foot, nearly causing him to fall. Regaining his balance, Jack looked down to see the perpetrator: a pair of discarded pruning shears. He shook his head and kicked them aside into the hedge, not wanting anyone else to trip.

A shrill scream erupted from nearby and Jack heard the frantic footsteps advancing on him before the couple came into view. They were young, early twenties by Jack's assumption, faces pale with terror. The man was holding the woman by the shoulders as though he had been pulling her away from whatever nightmare had struck fear into them.

"What is it?" Jack asked.

The woman pointed and screamed again. Jack approached, looking down the path. There was nothing to see but more hedges.

"Around the corner," the woman shouted. "Over there."

Jack took a step forward, but the man put a hand on his shoulder. Jack turned and saw him searching for the right words.

Be careful?

Don't go?

Then the woman steered the man back in the direction they had come from, pulling Jack along with them. "This way," she said.

As Jack followed them around the corner, the sight that had imbued the couple with horror came into view. A woman lay motionless on the stone path, her shoulders propped up against the hedge. Her legs were splayed, frozen amid a brutal struggle. Blood drained out of a gaping wound in her throat, saturating into the ripped maid's uniform. Her head was hanging back, the crown half hidden inside the hedge wall. Jack recognized her instantly.

"Go get help!" he shouted at the couple.

They didn't move, petrified in place.

"Go! Get the police!"

As they scampered off, Jack knelt down, mindful not to touch the dead woman's body. He wanted to reach out and pull her head up straight, look into her eyes to confirm she was truly gone and that there was nothing he could do to help, but he knew how foolish that was. Of course, she was already dead. Her neck was torn open like the lid of a tin can.

He stood shouting up into the sky for help. *"I'm in the rose garden. Someone's been killed! Call the police!"*

It wasn't until the crowd arrived — most of which was made up by the people he'd seen at the cabana bar — that Jack finally stopped yelling for aid. They circled around him, gawking at the slain woman, murmuring and whispering. Some of them gave Jack suspicious looks, others focused solely on Monica's body, while some still appeared unfazed by the whole scene and were ready to return to their cocktails.

"Why are you all just standing there?" Jack shouted. *"Get the police!"*

Chapter 16
Inspector Righetti's Interrogation

Jack sat in Inspector Righetti's office, outside of which lingered an army of police officers, glaring in at him, their thoughts already made up regarding his involvement in the crime. Righetti sat across the desk, his eyes bloodshot from being awakened in the middle of the night.

"Why are you in Sicily?"

"We already went over this," Jack said.

"Tell me again."

"I'm here for vacation on my employer's dime."

"And who's your employer?"

Jack sighed with hesitation before responding. "He's an American politician."

Righetti snorted. "American politics repulse me."

"I feel the same."

"Yet you don't mind profiting from them," Righetti said.

"I profit from them. That doesn't mean they don't bother me. Am I here to talk about my boss or about the woman who was found murdered?"

"We've been dancing this waltz for a few days now, haven't we? And with each attack, your face gets brought up repeatedly."

"Well, when you're staying at a resort that's the target of a crazed killer, I suppose that's bound to happen."

Righetti took a sip of his coffee. "It was reported that you were talking to the recently deceased Monica Bruno just earlier today. The resort concierge said he saw her leaving your room in distress."

Earlier today? What time was it? Wasn't that yesterday by now? Jack bit his cheek. He contemplated sharing that the concierge was also seemingly running an escort service in his spare time, but knew it wouldn't help in this circumstance.

"This is now the second victim you've been seen with prior to their murder," Righetti said.

"You make it sound like I was the only person in the whole resort that she interacted with. Surely you realize how ridiculous that sounds."

"Why was she distressed leaving your room? And why was she in your room to begin with?" Righetti asked.

"I was just asking her questions."

"About what?"

"About a... suspect."

"Oh, you have suspects now? Excuse me, I didn't realize you'd joined my police force. When did you enlist?"

"There's a resort employee, an attendant—"

"No, no, no," Righetti said. "You explain to me first why you think you have the privilege of conducting your own investigation into this case."

"Look, I've got a lead. You want to hear the information I have or not?"

"Depends how credible it is."

"Marco Marino. He's an attendant at the resort. He's got a clear motive."

"Oh, really?" Righetti said smugly. "And what's that?"

"The Black Brigade killed his family during the war. Vittoria Gaeta and the cook, Illaria, were both attacked with a military dagger, the same type the Black Brigade used. And—"

"What was that?" Righetti asked, straightening up. "How the hell would you know what type of dagger was used to kill Vittoria Gaeta? That information hasn't been made public."

Jack looked at the officers glaring in from the other side of the glass. "Your men have big mouths, Inspector. The resort bartender overheard them talking about the case when he went to visit Illaria at the hospital."

Righetti didn't respond, but Jack knew from his body language that the notion of loose-lipped cops was equally infuriating, as it was unsurprising.

"Both women were daughters of Blackshirts," Jack continued. "I think the attacks were revenge for Marco's family. That's why he left the dagger at the crime scene. To send a message. My guess is Monica was the daughter of a Blackshirt as well."

"Almost everyone in Italy is a descendant of someone who served in the fascist regime. Why target these women specifically?"

For the first time, Jack didn't have an answer.

"And there was no dagger found near Monica Bruno's body," Righetti said. "The method of killing was quite different. Pruning shears."

Pruning shears?

Jack thought back to the pair he had tripped on in the rose garden. He'd stepped on the murder weapon and not even realized it.

"So perhaps her murder was committed by someone else entirely," Righetti said. "A bitter foreigner perhaps?"

Jack sighed. "I can see why my association with the victims is suspicious, but I've got no motive for the killings. I have no connection to the Black Brigade. I didn't even fight in the war. I was too young."

"What about your family? *Your* father? He would have been of age to fight."

"He would've been, but he never had the opportunity to be drafted. He was murdered when I was a toddler. My life has been one of violence, Inspector, and I've been but a spectator the whole time. You asked why I'm doing my own investigation? I'm tired of just watching."

"If that's so, then it sounds like I need to ensure you don't continue to interfere with my case. Maybe I'll pair you up in a holding cell with Elio Gaeta. I'm sure the two of you will find plenty to discuss."

Jack leaned forward. "So Elio Gaeta *is* still in custody. Then he couldn't have attacked the other two women. So you think there are two killers."

An amused grin stretched across Righetti's face. "I have yet to rule anything out."

"Then don't rule out Marco. Look into him. He had an altercation with Monica at the pool before I spoke with her. She was terrified to tell me what it was about. The night Illaria was attacked, Monica said she saw someone — someone with a mask — burning clothing in the basement furnace."

"Easy to put words in a dead woman's mouth. I wonder why she wouldn't have come to the police if all that was true."

"Maybe you're unaware, but you don't have the best reputation around here."

"Of course. The police are the bad guys, right? Not the psychotic murderer butchering women."

"Look into Marco," Jack said.

Righetti sipped his coffee again and leaned back in his chair. He stared at Jack, analyzing him, then he waved for his partner, Gallo, on the other side of the glass.

Gallo pushed open the door and leaned inside. "Need me?"

Righetti responded without taking his sights off Jack. "Call the resort. Tell the manager we are going to need to speak to a Marco Marino."

"Marco Marino?" Gallo asked.

"He's an employee. Apparently, it might be worth our time to have a conversation with him."

"On it," Gallo said before hurrying off.

Righetti finished the last of his coffee. "What's the setup in the States when you get booked? One phone call, right?"

"Are you officially booking me, Inspector?" Jack asked.

"If I did, I assume you'd probably want to call that American politician employer of yours for help. But something tells me he's not coming anywhere near this little mess you've gotten yourself into. He'll just hang you out to dry. That's how it works over here, anyway. No one rescues anyone unless they get something out of it."

"Well, it's your turn to rescue someone, Inspector," Jack said. "Don't let Marco claim another victim. You get a paycheck. At the very least, *that's* what *you* get out of it."

Righetti chuckled. "You're so convinced this is the guy. Why? Because his family was killed? And so what, he just decides one day to knock off the daughters of fascists? Over twenty-five years later?"

"He just got hired. And then the murders started."

"You just showed up in town. And then the murders started. See how easy that is? And how do you know so much about this Marco, anyway? Breaking into the manager's office to rummage through the resort's personnel files?"

"One of the other employees—"

"Let me guess. The bartender. Same one who told you he overheard my men talking about the dagger at the hospital?"

Jack's expression betrayed him.

"That's what I thought," Righetti said. "You ever think this bartender has a grudge against Marco? Maybe the two of them don't get along at work, so he puts ideas in your head knowing you'd share them with me? Maybe the two of them were competing for the attention of one of the women who works there. The cook? The maid?"

Jack sunk back slowly into the chair as he considered Righetti's hypothesis. Luca *had* laid it all out, hadn't he? Was Jack being misled?

No. No, Jack had heard those strange words from Marco firsthand. What was it he said again?

It seems as though blood flows continuously here in Sicily. Sometimes it's from the veins you want, other times it's not. Accepting that is the only way one seems able to survive.

What the hell did that mean? Who the hell says something like that? Especially after such shocking attacks?

Yes, there was certainly something off about Marco. What Luca had said had only bolstered Jack's already blooming suspicions.

The office door opened again, and Gallo leaned inside. "Manager says Marco Marino didn't show up for his shift. They haven't heard from him."

Righetti stood. "And he didn't think that was worth reporting? A staff member failing to show up the morning after another was brutally murdered on resort grounds?"

"Guess not," Gallo said with a shrug.

"Have someone go over there and pull the man's file. And call that damn manager back to get his address. I want to pay this guy a visit at home."

Gallo nodded before retreating from the office once more.

As he pulled on his jacket, Righetti looked down at Jack, still seated in the chair. "And you—"

"Let me guess," Jack said. "Stay close?"

Chapter 17
Visiting Hours

Illaria Conti laid in the hospital bed, staring out the window at the sea. She felt lucky to have such a beautiful view during her recovery, but more so, she felt lucky to be alive. The knife wound below her shoulder had been cleaned, stitched and bandaged, and was now concealed by the hospital gown she wore. She'd been told that today they would discharge her, and she could do the rest of her recovery at home. With her attacker still on the loose, leaving the security of the hospital made her apprehensive. The presence of the police officer stationed outside her door was the only solace she had.

The medication she'd been given made it difficult to organize her thoughts as she replayed the events of the attack in her head. The slash of the dagger. The pop of the lightbulbs. The silhouette of the hat and raincoat. As the visuals bombarded her, she asked herself the same three questions over and over.

Who was he?

Why had he attacked her?

Where was he now?

She hoped the police had some answers, or at least a few clues that could lead them to answers. And soon.

Maybe he had just been some random madman. A stranger who'd snuck into the resort that targeted her for no other reason than the ease of it, because she was alone and out of sight. The world had its share of crazies, and the resort wasn't any kind of fortress designed to keep them out. Sure, they had security personnel, but anyone with half a care could easily evade them.

Who was he? A random madman.

Why had he attacked her? She seemed like easy prey.

Where was he now?

That was the most concerning question, wasn't it? Aside from identity and motive, the most urgent puzzle that needed solving was her attacker's whereabouts. Was he still lurking about the resort, ready to attack some other unsuspecting staff member? Had he fled the country, worried that Illaria could somehow identify him? Or was he standing outside her room at this very moment, having already slit the throat of the police officer? Dread washed over her once more as the worst possible scenarios overtook her focus.

A knock at the door brought her to attention, and she pulled herself up in bed. "Yes?"

Luca leaned his head in through the doorway. "Mind if I come in?"

Illaria smiled. "Of course not." She waved him inside.

"How're you feeling?" he asked, taking a seat in the chair beside the bed.

"Not terrible. How's the chef? Is he upset that I've missed so much work?"

"Don't be ridiculous. Everyone's just thankful you weren't killed."

Illaria nodded, her gaze drifting. Luca could tell she was sinking into another wave of dark thoughts.

"They'll catch him soon," he said, trying to pull her back out. "You don't have to be afraid."

Her eyes found him again. "I hope that's true."

Luca struggled to think of a way to steer the conversation in a more cheerful direction. "How's the food here?"

Illaria grinned and shook her head. "Absolutely dreadful."

"Really? I'm surprised they don't have the culinary world's top cooks on staff."

She laughed. "Not quite."

"Good. Then I don't have to worry about them trying to steal you away."

"You wouldn't like that?"

"If you left the resort to work somewhere else? Of course not. Who would I tease at the end of my shift every night if you weren't there?"

"Is that your way of saying you'd miss me?"

"Yeah. That's my way of saying I'd miss you."

Illaria grinned. "I'd miss you too."

"And I still owe you dinner. Don't think I've forgotten."

"Oh yeah? Where are we going to go?"

"Wherever you want."

"I've heard good things about Malfatti's."

Luca nodded. "Malfatti's it is then."

"Or Pigozzi's is always good."

"No, I think Malfatti's. It's fancier."

"You want to take me some place fancy, eh?" Illaria asked playfully.

"I do indeed."

"I'm sure they've got some superb cooks *there*."

"Yeah, I'd imagine they do," Luca said.

"I've got that test coming up in a few weeks, you know? If I do well, the chef might move me out of prep. I'd get to work alongside the real pros."

Luca put his hand on Illaria's atop the railing of the hospital bed. "That'll be something to celebrate."

The two of them talked for a while longer, Luca doing his best to raise her spirits, Illaria fully aware of his intentions. Then Luca bid her goodbye, saying he needed to head into work for his shift. As he moved to the door, he asked if he could come by her house tomorrow to check on her once she'd been released from the hospital. Illaria said she appreciated it, but that her sister, Valentina, was coming in from Rome to stay with her for a few days to help sort things out.

"She gets in later tonight," Illaria said.

"Looking forward to meeting her at some point. Until next time."

"Until next time," Illaria echoed.

Luca departed, leaving Illaria with a swell of positivity. The image of her attacker, which had been plaguing her since that fateful night, was drowned beneath a wave of hope. She played out a scenario in her head of Luca arriving at her door to pick her up. He'd be charming, as usual, and her sister would be smitten. He'd escort her down the steps to his Fiat, opening the door for her and helping her inside. They'd drive through town, the nightlife of Sicily awaiting them, offering a myriad of adventures to choose from. The glow of Terme del Paradiso on the coast would be a reminder of the culinary test she'd soon undertake, but it wouldn't be a cause for stress. It would be a source of excitement. Of a new opportunity. Her dream becoming reality.

Pulling up outside Malfatti's, Luca would put the car in park, then hurry around to open the door for her once more. The doorman would welcome them inside and the grandeur of the restaurant — which she'd previously only glimpsed through the windows while walking past — would radiate with such magnificence that the two of them would have to pause in place to endure it. A hostess would lead them to the table Luca had reserved, and a perfectly dressed waiter would arrive to share all the best dishes the chef had prepared.

Illaria would glance around the room, seeing familiar faces. Not friends. Not co-workers. It would be the guests of Terme del Paradiso, those rich elites who had the luxury of dining in such a fine establishment regularly, as though it were no more special than an average corner café. In a way, she would feel sorry for them, because they don't appreciate all that Malfatti's truly offers. It wouldn't be a special occasion for them. Just dinner. Just a normal night out. But for Illaria, it would be everything. A chance to taste renowned cuisine. To be waited on. Taken care of. And an opportunity to spend time outside of work with Luca. Nothing could ruin such a night for her.

When the food arrives, she would do her best to identify the ingredients, guess at the process. Like a sommelier sharing tasting notes, she would explain the complexities to Luca. Garlic. Basil. She imagined this wouldn't annoy him. He'd enjoy it. He'd enjoy hearing her speak passionately about something she loved. Maybe he'd even ask her questions, to elaborate more, and share the details of such an exquisitely crafted meal. They would taste and talk and savor and share.

And there would be wine. God, yes, there would be wine. It would be paired, of course, hand-selected by the owner, a celebrated expert in the worlds of both Italian wine and cuisine. Each course would be matched with its own vintage, the flavors complimenting one another marvelously. The alcohol would slowly remove any nervousness either of them had, the jitters of a first date.

As the waiter clears whatever ambrosian dessert is served, Luca would ask for the bill, but the waiter replies that it has already been taken care of. He'd gesture to another table, where a wealthy couple is sitting. They are guests at Terme del Paradiso, ones who Luca had provided exemplary service to in the resort lounge over the past week. Luca and Illaria would thank them for their generosity, and the couple would tell Illaria that Luca is the best bartender in all of Sicily. Luca won't be able to keep from blushing.

Back in his Fiat, they'd drive through town toward Illaria's place. He'd steal a look at her every so often, and she'd tell him to keep his eyes on the road. Outside her home, he'd walk her up to the door. They'd pause awkwardly before Illaria makes the first move, leaning in just enough for Luca's doubt to fade. Then he'd kiss her.

Her sister, Valentina, would be just inside the door when she enters, asking for all the details, peering out the window at Luca as he gets back into his Fiat and cruises away.

"He's a handsome one," Valentina would say.

They'd sit together on the couch, and Illaria would recant the events of the evening. Still lost in the cloud of euphoria, her lifeblood, the wine, pumping out all the self-doubt and second-guessing, Illaria would ride the wave of bliss until she falls asleep.

There in the hospital bed, she smiled widely, her eyes closed. Soon things would be better. Soon, things may even be exactly like that. A lovely date. A safe place to lay her head. In a way, she'd not really felt safe since her grandfather had passed. He had been her security blanket as much as he was her mentor. With him gone, she felt alone. And she *was* alone in most respects. She lived alone. She worked the overnight shifts in the kitchen alone. She even walked home alone. And while sometimes it made her feel brave and mature, mostly it made her feel forgotten.

Forgotten by the remaining fragments of her family.

Maybe this visit from her sister would be exactly what she'd been needing. It was unfortunate that it took her getting attacked for Valentina to look in on her, but Illaria accepted that life was full of harsh realities.

Opening her eyes, she faced the door. As quickly as the anxiety had dissipated, it crept back. She couldn't help but wonder if the officer was still out there. Should she call to him just to be sure? She'd feel silly as soon as she did it, of course. Like a child calling to their parent in the other room just to be sure a monster hadn't eaten them.

No, she was safe here. She was protected.

For now.

Chapter 18
The Home Of Marco Marino

Alberto Marino brushed past the drying bedsheets strung up across the alley as he walked home. Dogs and chickens shared the play space with neighborhood children, all of them moving aside as he came through. The smell of the fish market permeated the air, and the shouts of a street vendor selling cockles called again and again, repeating like waves upon the shore. For as long as he could remember, every day had felt the same. The sights, the smells, the sounds. Hopeless monotony. But today was different. Today Alberto felt alive. He felt powerful. He felt as though he'd just set his life on a new course.

The memory prodded at him. The gun in his hand. The ringing in his ears. The dead body crumpled on the floor, blood spreading across the tile. His first job for the mafia had been a success. Trust, cash and more opportunity would no doubt follow. He'd need to keep it all from his cousin, Marco, of course. He wouldn't understand. And he wouldn't approve. Marco had moved in with him only a few weeks back, and already found himself a legitimate job at Terme del Paradiso. If he knew Alberto had resorted to doing dirty jobs for mafiosos, there would be no end to the shaming. The fewer people who knew of it, the better anyway.

Loose lips sink ships, as the saying went. And Alberto had no intention of drowning.

It was only seconds after entering his home and setting down his things on the kitchen table he heard a rap at the door.

"*Mr Marino?*" The voice was aggressive. Authoritarian. No one ever called him Mr Marino. He was just Alberto. Alberto to everyone who knew him anyhow.

Another knock at the door.

"*Mr Marino, my name is Inspector Righetti. We'd like to speak with you about an urgent matter.*"

Inspector? The goddamned police. What possible urgent matter would the police need to speak with him about?

"*Mr Marino, we saw you enter. We know you're inside. Please come to the door.*"

Alberto knew there was only one reason they'd be here. Someone must have seen him murder that butcher. Someone must have ratted him out. His first job for the mafia, and he'd botched it. How could he have been so stupid? How could he have let himself get caught? He'd been so careful. The blinds had been pulled, the door locked. He'd come in through the back and put a bullet in the old man's head before the poor bastard even had time to turn around. Then, as quickly as he'd come, he had disappeared into the darkness of the alley, face covered in a bandana for good measure.

The knocking grew more violent, a heavy fist pounding against the wood. "*Mr Marino! Do not make me ask again. Open the door!*"

With no time to spare, he marched into the kitchen and pulled out the silverware drawer from the cabinet, dumping its contents onto the floor and removing the false bottom where he'd hidden the pistol. Forks and spoons danced across the room, their jingle exposing his panic to the cops on the other side of the door.

"What do you want?" Alberto's voice cracked into a shrill wail.

"*We just need to speak with you.*"

"What about?"

"Don't make me keep shouting through this door. Just open up."

"I don't wanna talk right now," Alberto said, his sweaty hands wrapped around the pistol grip.

"This is the last time I'm going to ask, then I'm kicking the door in!"

Alberto raised the pistol and took aim.

"Don't you fucking come in here!"

He backed up against the kitchen counter, his sights set, hands shaking. The ceiling creaked, his upstairs neighbors moving about, no doubt going to their window to get a better look at the police outside. He wished there was a back door he could escape through just like he had at the butcher shop, but the only way in or out was through the alley where the inspector now stood.

When he had gone to kill the butcher, his biggest worry was whether he'd be able to follow through with it, whether he'd fail and in doing so get himself marked for death by the men who had hired him. Now, there was no question of death. It was a certainty. The police had come for him, and whether they gunned him down here in his home, or arrested him and beat him to death in a holding cell, Alberto knew that an entry-level mafia thug hung out to dry would get no mercy from an Inspector who'd seen more than his share of innocents killed by mafiosos.

As the inevitability of his untimely end settled in, Alberto's hands steadied. If this was to be the conclusion to his story, he was going to do his best to make it one hell of a finale.

Moments earlier, Inspector Righetti entered the alley with his partner, Gallo, approaching the address of Marco Marino.

"How many more attacks can the resort bear before people pile out in droves?" Gallo asked.

"The people who can afford to stay there don't concern themselves with the trouble of others. As long as they get their fancy meals and massages, they couldn't care less about a few dead bodies."

"Well, if there *have* to be dead bodies, I prefer them to keep popping up *there*. I wouldn't mind spending more time at the resort, that's for certain. Each crime scene's been like a little taste of the rich life, you know?"

It was a crude sentiment, but Righetti understood what his partner was trying to say.

"That's not the real world, Gallo. Don't get lost in the fantasy."

"Real or not, I'd kill to stay there. Did you taste the pomegranate juice? What the hell do they put in that stuff?"

"Pomegranate, I suppose."

"Pomegranate and rich bitch blood," Gallo said.

Righetti stopped and stared at his partner.

Gallo halted and looked back at him, and reading the concern in the Inspector's face, shrugged and grinned. "That was just a way to say that they've got elegance flowing in their veins. It was good fucking juice. And the women there. My God. Walking around dressed in—"

"*Yes!*" Righetti shouted, his patience disintegrating. "*Yes*, the women are beautiful. Lounging half-naked by the pool, drinking their wine, laughing at their boyfriends' jokes. All the guests look like royalty, waited on by an army of perfectly dressed servants. The views are gorgeous. It's the same beach, the same fucking ocean, and yet somehow, from the vantage point of Terme del Paradiso, they look even grander. And *yes*, the fucking pomegranate juice tastes like heaven. Now, if you're quite done romanticizing about a life you'll never live, we have a goddamn job to do."

Righetti started walking again. Embarrassed, Gallo followed along beside him.

As they turned down a perpendicular alley, they saw a man enter one of the homes. Gallo checked the address he'd inked onto his wrist.

"Inspector. That's it right there."

They watched as the man went inside.

"Son of a bitch. Perfect fucking timing," Righetti said.

They hurried over. Righetti knocked.

"Mr Marino?" They waited, then Righetti knocked again. "Mr Marino, my name is Inspector Righetti. We'd like to speak with you about an urgent matter."

No response. Gallo shook his head. "Bastard thinks he can ignore us."

Righetti knocked harder this time. "Mr Marino! Do not make me ask again. Open the door!"

They could hear the man moving around inside, then something crashed on the floor.

"He's panicking," Gallo said.

"What do you want?" the man's voice finally responded.

"We just need to speak with you," Righetti answered.

"What about?"

"This ballsy son of a bitch," Righetti muttered to himself. He had no tolerance for defiance, especially not from a murder suspect. "Don't make me keep shouting through this door! Just open up."

"I don't wanna talk right now."

Did he think it was a request? They were the police. If the bastard didn't want to get his jaw cracked with the butt of Righetti's pistol, he'd be smart to do as he's told.

"This is the last time I'm going to ask," Righetti called. "Then I'm kicking the door in!"

"Don't you fucking come in here!" The man's voice sounded frantic. Dangerous.

"Inspector?" Gallo said, ready for whatever direction would follow.

Righetti pulled his pistol. Gallo followed suit.

Above them, an old woman stepped out onto the balcony and peered down curiously.

"Go back inside," Gallo said, waving her away.

She raised her eyebrows and pursed her lips, offended by the young policeman's rude behavior.

"Back inside," he hissed.

She sneered before acquiescing.

Gallo turned to Righetti, who was waiting for his partner's attention.

"Ready?"

Gallo nodded.

Righetti motioned at the door and moved aside. Gallo took a step back, then kicked as hard as he could. The frail door cracked at the hinges and swung open wide. Righetti dropped to one knee and pointed his pistol.

"Marino!"

There was no one in sight, the room empty, a mess of silverware scattered across the floor. Gallo slid through the doorway, his sidearm up and ready. Righetti waited until Gallo found cover near the sofa, then he stood and strafed in, his aim bouncing between the kitchen space and the closed bedroom door.

"Marino, come on out. We just need to talk."

Gallo checked behind the overturned kitchen table, kicking the emptied drawer out of his way. He clocked the knife holder on the counter, the empty slot glaringly obvious.

"We don't want anyone hurt here, Marino. Let's avoid any accidents and settle for a calm conversation." Righetti cocked his head, and Gallo went to the bedroom door, sidling up along the wall within arm's reach of the doorknob.

The cluck of a startled chicken drew their attention back to the front door. A child, no older than ten, stood before the shattered frame, staring in at the Inspector and his partner. Gallo waved him away as he had the old woman on the balcony. The child remained, staring blankly at the two men.

"*Go!*" Gallo whispered.

The boy didn't move.

"Marino?" Righetti called. "You're making this more difficult than it needs to."

A chicken strutted into view in the front doorway beside the boy and the child scooped it up, cradling it in his arms like a puppy.

"*I know what you want!*" The man's voice finally said from inside the bedroom.

Gallo waved at the boy again, desperately urging him to leave.

"Yeah?" Righetti replied, his pistol trained on the bedroom door, ready for whatever may happen next. "And what's that?"

"*Me. Dead.*"

"And why would we want you dead, Marino?"

"Isn't that what you do to men like me?"

Gallo looked to Righetti, who motioned for him to take care of the situation at the front door. Hurrying over, Gallo gently forced the child away, sending him further down the alley.

"We're not executioners. Just here to talk. Now please, come out of the bedroom," Righetti said.

Gallo returned to the bedroom door. They waited as a long, silent moment passed.

"If you're not coming out, then we're coming in. And if you aren't standing in the middle of the room with your hands empty and raised, I guarantee you this won't go well."

"Fuck you!"

"Enough of this," Righetti growled. Then to Gallo he said, "Do it."

Gallo turned the knob and pushed the door open, leaning back quickly to give the Inspector a clear view. A flame spun out of the darkness, twisting through the air, hurtling toward Righetti. The bottom edge of the Molotov cocktail caught the left side of the doorframe and the bottle shattered, casting an explosion of hellfire across the room. Shards of glass peppered Righetti, and he pulled the trigger of his pistol in response.

"Christ!"

Gunshots from inside the bedroom screamed through the spreading flames. Shielding his face, Gallo returned fire, squeezing off three shots, stepping backward with each one to distance himself from the growing inferno.

Righetti took cover behind the sofa, popping up to shoot at the assailant. The clicking of an empty chamber from inside the bedroom told him all he needed to know. He stood and, through the collecting smoke, could make out the shape of the man inside. Taking calculated aim, he steadied his breathing and fired.

The man squealed and doubled over.

"Gallo," Righetti said, coming out from behind the sofa. "With me." He approached the doorway, taking a moment to work up his nerve before leaping through the flames. The man lay on the floor, a bullet hole in his chest. He was still alive, but fading fast.

"Goddamn you, Marco," Righetti said, kicking the empty pistol out of the man's reach.

Even through the smoke, Righetti could see the confusion spread across the dying man's face. He wheezed, blood leaking from his mouth, and sputtered out, *"Marco?"*

Chapter 19
The Pleasure Of Pinocchio

Silvia's hand carved through the water, scooping it backward, propelling her forward through the pool. Her head turned to the side, stealing air from the surface before dipping back below. From one end of the pool to the other, she stroked gracefully, unburdened by the presence of anyone else. The media had been at the resort all day, snapping photos, interviewing staff, trying their best to dig up tiny details about the attacks to plaster the papers with. While the other guests were engaging with the press, indulging in their fifteen minutes of fame, or had otherwise retreated to their rooms for solitude to get away from the chaos, the pool had become Silvia's own private escape.

Memories of her father (from when he was a much younger man, and she but a child) stabbed at her as she swam. She was sitting on the floor beside her parents' bed, playing with her doll as he paced about, her mother in the kitchen pretending to listen to the words that had echoed in their house for years. His rage had peeled its way out of the professional facade, and he ranted about the embarrassment the country had become, having abandoned its ideals by switching sides during the war. He complained about the mafia, how Mussolini's fascists had imprisoned them in Sicily, and that it was the allied forces, when they landed on the island during the war, who set them all free to continue their criminal enterprise.

A knock at the door signaled the arrival of two men which, until that time, Silvia had only seen in the old photograph her mother kept on her nightstand beside the bed. They were slightly older than in the picture, and maybe a bit heavier, but their eyes were unmistakable. They greeted her parents and sat down with her father in the living room while her mother prepared coffee.

Keeping out of sight, Silvia listened to the conversation, failing to understand the context of most of it, but latching on to certain fragments, most notably when one of the men said, "Conti survived the war only to eat a bullet now."

Eat a bullet.

It was a disgusting image that only became more horrible as she learned later what it actually meant.

"How things are, and how things should be, are always so far apart," her father said.

They sipped their coffee until the daylight waned and then they pulled out the wine, at which point Silvia's mother took her into the bedroom where they sat and read from one of her story books.

"Those are the men from your photograph," Silvia said, sitting on her mother's lap.

"They are," her mother replied. "They fought in the war with your father. Carlo Rossini and Fabio Cairo. They're good men."

"They look sad."

"That's because they *are* a bit sad, Silvia."

"Why?"

"A good friend of theirs passed away."

"Oh. Were they happy before that?"

Her mother paused. "No, Silvia. They've not been happy for a long time, I'm afraid. There is much sadness in this world."

"Because we lost the war?"

"That's right. And because the more time that passes, the more that men like your father and his friends will be vilified for the brave things they did. This country has turned against them. And to be shunned by your own country is a very painful thing to endure."

Silvia gripped the rails and climbed out of the pool, the memory washing away with the water. She slipped on her sandals and toweled herself off, wringing out her hair.

"My God, you're beautiful," a voice said from behind, startling Silvia, who turned to see a woman in a sandy cream-colored crochet swim cover-up that she wore over a white bikini.

"Oh. Thank you," Silvia said, covering up with the towel.

"Sorry if me saying so is awkward. I've seen you around the resort a few times and I keep wanting to run up and tell you, but I didn't want you to think I was a psychopath or something like that."

Silvia blushed, wrapping the towel around herself properly. "You're too kind, honestly. And coming from you, it's quite the compliment. You're absolutely gorgeous."

She grinned. "I'm Ellie, by the way."

"Silvia. You're American I take it?"

"Bingo! My husband and I have been touring all over Italy. We saw Rome, and Florence, and Naples before coming here. *God*, Naples."

"Lovely. I hope it's been memorable."

"It's been quite the experience."

"Well, enjoy the pool. Beautiful day for it." Silvia smiled and turned to head inside.

"You're leaving?" Ellie asked in a disappointed tone.

Silvia paused and looked back. "Yes, I got my workout in for the day."

"That's a shame. I was hoping for some company. Everyone seems to be a bit skittish today. Understandably, of course. But as I told my husband, I will let nothing ruin this trip for us."

"Good mentality to have. He's not coming out to join you?"

Hands on her hips, Ellie looked out at the ocean past the pool, surveying the horizon as a form of punctuation. "No, he's up in the room, hoping I return soon with some company." She turned back to Silvia. "You're here alone?"

Silvia tilted her head, unsure if she understood the insinuation.

"I am."

"You may have gotten your workout in for the day, but my husband and I are just getting ready for ours. Our next one, anyway. Can't ever get enough exercise, am I right?" She bit her lip, coyly raising her eyebrows with a look of anticipation.

THE HEAVY CURTAINS WERE DRAWN, blocking out the sunlight. Silvia admired the splendor of the hotel suite. It was much more spacious than her room, with a central lounge area separate from a pair of bedrooms and a lavish bathroom.

"Pour yourself a drink if you'd like," Ellie said, gesturing toward the globe bar behind the sofa. "I'll let George know I'm back." Then she sauntered off into one of the bedrooms.

Once alone, Silvia immediately considered leaving, unsure if her decision to accompany the woman she'd only just met for a ménage à trois was wise. If she were going to flee, now was the time. But she desperately needed the distraction, and if she couldn't cleanse herself of the plaguing memories with a dip in the pool, then perhaps this unexpected escapade would do the trick.

She listened to the hushed voices of Ellie and who she assumed to be Ellie's husband, George, unable to make out much of anything being said. Only snippets escaped to find her.

... gorgeous.

... mouth...

... pool.

Then clearly she heard Ellie say, "You're going to fucking love her."

Seizing the burst of confidence, Silvia discarded her towel and walked over to the bar in nothing but her bikini. She grabbed the J&B bottle by the neck and let the whisky cascade into a collins glass.

When Ellie emerged from the bedroom, Silvia saw she had swapped her poolside attire for a black leather corset, stiletto boots and a black veil, the type she'd seen nuns wear, complete with the stark white band across the brow. A crucifix rested between her breasts, and she held a riding crop, which dangled beside her leg.

Silvia took a healthy swig of the whisky. "Love the outfit."

"Come here," Ellie said, raising the crop so that it gently slapped against her breast, jostling the crucifix.

Silvia set her glass down inside the globe bar and approached.

"I didn't realize we were playing dress up. Do you have something for me to wear?"

Ellie tucked a stray bit of hair behind Silvia's ear. "You won't be needing anything."

Silvia followed Ellie into the second bedroom, where a four-poster bed awaited.

"Remove your bikini and lie down," she said.

Silvia did as she was told.

"I'm going to tie you to the bed now. Is that all right?"

Tie me down? How many kinks does this woman have, Silvia wondered.

She nodded and allowed Ellie to do as she wanted.

Using leather straps, Ellie secured Silvia's wrists and ankles to the corners of the bed, sensually kissing her arms and legs along the way. From the nightstand, she revealed a ball gag that she gently placed into Silvia's mouth before fastening the belt around the back of her head.

It was then that a startling figure stepped in through the doorway. He wore a black leather mask with a zipper mouth and two holes cut out for his green eyes. The nose was a long black dildo that jiggled as he approached, making him look like some perverted version of Pinocchio. With the exception of the mask, he was naked. His body fit, his penis flaccid. In his hand, he held a black leather briefcase, which he set down at the end of the bed between Silvia's spread legs. He opened it; the lid concealing whatever mysteries lie inside.

Ellie walked around behind and slapped him on the ass with the riding crop. Silvia could hear the man gasp behind the mask.

"Say hello to our guest, George."

George groaned. Or growled. Silvia wasn't sure which.

He reached inside the briefcase, but Ellie slapped him again, and he yelped.

"Tell her how beautiful she is."

The green eyes scoured every inch of Silvia's naked body, and George moaned in pleasure as though he were already inside her.

"That's better," Ellie said.

George looked at his wife as if for approval.

"Mmm. Not quite yet. Let's save that for the finale, shall we, baby?"

George looked back at the briefcase, then at Silvia, then back at the briefcase. Finally, he closed it up and set it on the dinette table. Returning to the end of the bed, George climbed up onto the mattress like some great, lumbering beast. He straddled over Silvia, his limp dick dragging across her stomach.

Silvia looked up into his green eyes.

He slowly leaned down toward her and the tip of the dildo nose prodded the ball gag in her mouth.

"Oh, no," Ellie said playfully. "Looks like there's no entry permitted there. How ever will you get inside, my love?"

Ellie's hand slid in-between them, grabbed hold of George's cock and stroked it until it grew hard. Silvia could feel the pre-cum wet her naval as Ellie directed the head of his penis teasingly."Not there either," she said.

George backed down further, kneeling between Silvia's legs like a deviant clown at church.

"Here?" Ellie asked. "Yes, that will probably work."

She slid up onto the bed beside Silvia, nuzzling her head against Silvia's shoulder.

"What do you say? Can I let my husband fuck you there?"

Silvia could feel her heart pounding in her chest. She nodded.

Ellie wet her fingers in her mouth, then prepared Silvia to receive her husband. George grabbed Silvia's ass cheeks and lifted as he entered her aggressively. Silvia gasped, feeling him deeper with every thrust. As he went harder, faster, Ellie slapped him repeatedly in the face with the riding crop, some of the blows hitting his leather-clad cheeks, others the dildo nose, causing it to wobble comically.

Then Ellie stood on the bed, her legs on either side of Silvia, and leaned forward to hold the headboard for balance, presenting her ass to her husband.

"My turn, baby."

Silvia strained to watch as George began bobbing his head like a chicken, the dildo nose penetrating his wife with every forward motion.

This was all too bizarre for Silvia. She expected a threesome, not an S&M vaudeville show. What the fuck was going on?

"Don't you cum in her!" Ellie shouted at George between her moans of pleasure. *"Don't you fucking cum in her, baby!"*

She stared down at Silvia as she braced herself against the headboard.

"You like that, you little slut? You like getting fucked by a married man?"

If she handn't been strapped down to the bed, Silvia may have jumped up and ran for the door. But the cuffs held her in place, and the gag kept her from telling Ellie she'd had enough.

"Tell me you like it," Ellie said. "Say, uh huh. Uh huh, I like it, Ellie!"

Silvia shook her head.

Ellie slapped her across the cheek with the riding crop. "Say, uh huh!"

Silvia's teeth bit down into the gag, her anger reaching its peak.

"Say it!"

Though the oddities of the encounter were undeniable, and far more outlandish than she had expected, Silvia couldn't deny that whatever terrible memories she was trying to forget had long since vanished from her mind.

"Uh huh. Uh huh," Silvia breathed past the gag.

"You like getting fucked by my husband?"

"Uh huh!"

George moaned through the mask and Ellie, who could tell he was about to explode, shouted, *"Cum on her tits, baby! I wanna lick it off!"*

George pulled out, and Silvia felt the splatter of warmth across her torso. Ellie pulled herself away from her husband's face and Silvia saw the gleaming dildo nose jiggle free, slinging Ellie's juices in an arc across the bed. Ellie splayed herself atop Silvia, her tongue lapping up the spilt seed.

George backed off the edge of the bed and went to the briefcase, propping it open once more. Silvia turned her head, trying her best to see what the contents were, but her attention quickly returned to Ellie, who began kissing her neck.

Silvia's body tingled. She felt Ellie's fingers inside her, then her tongue. The handcuffs were tantalizingly frustrating, restricting her movements, forcing her to lie helpless, unable to be an active participant in the game. She wanted to grab Ellie by the hair, force her face harder against her flesh, bury her mouth deep inside. But she couldn't break free.

A prisoner on the bed.

Paralyzed.

She closed her eyes, drifting into a state of ecstasy as Ellie's tongue coiled around each nerve ending like a serpent examining its nest. The vibration of Ellie's excited laugh brought her to climax, and when Silvia finally opened her eyes again, she saw what had elicited the woman's giggle.

George stood beside the bed, having removed the coveted item from the briefcase. The long, smooth blade of the dagger rested in the palm of his hand. He pinched it between his thumb and index finger, rubbing up and down the length of the metal. His green eyes were wide with anticipation, two frighteningly handsome orbs existing within the slick leather mask. Silvia tried to scream, but the ball gag in her mouth reduced the sound to a muffled, wet spurt.

"This is the finale," Ellie said as she hopped up and over Silvia, settling in behind her like a coach in Lamaze class.

Silvia thrashed, trying desperately to break free of the handcuffs as George crept back up onto the mattress between her legs.

"Isn't she beautiful, baby? Don't you just wanna fuck this Italian bitch till she's dead?"

"Uh huh," George said through the mask. Each breath he took

sounded damp, as if the sweat from his exhaustion had accumulated inside, ready to drown him. He pointed the tip of the dagger at Silvia, inching it closer as she struggled to escape.

"Settle down. Settle down," Ellie said as she cupped her hands around Silvia's eyes. "You don't want him to miss."

Silvia felt something penetrate her, and she screamed through the gag. The phallic instrument moved in and out rhythmically, yet there was no pain. Ellie removed her hands and Silvia saw George was fucking her with the dildo nose, the dagger safely set aside.

What the fuck!

Silvia bucked her hips, knocking him back off the bed and onto his ass on the floor. She flailed dramatically, shouting at Ellie as best she could to prove she was no longer enjoying herself.

"Christ! Calm down! It's just a game!"

Ellie got out from beneath her, grabbed the knife, and slammed it back inside the briefcase.

"It's just for the thrill! Jesus! Calm the fuck down! I thought you'd be good with it!"

Silvia's wrathful face told her otherwise.

George pulled off the mask and tossed it aside. "Are you okay?"

"Uhn uh!" Silvia said.

"Okay, okay." He uncuffed her ankles, then her wrists.

Silvia sat up and ripped the gag from her mouth. "You people are insane!"

George turned to Ellie. "You said she was into it."

"I thought she would be!"

"Well, she's not!"

"She seemed like she was until you pulled out the knife, *George!*"

"The knife is the whole thing, *Ellie!*"

"Fuck you people," Silvia said, storming from the bedroom and pulling on her bikini in the process.

"You already did," Ellie quipped.

"I'm sorry," George said, following her into the living room.

Silvia turned and saw he had the dagger in his hand. "Stay the fuck away from me," she warned.

"Just — let me explain. You see, we've got what you might call a morbid fantasy, and—"

"Oh yes, I see that," Silvia shot back.

"You were never in any danger. I would never—"

"What? Fuck me with a knife?"

"Right! I would never fuck you with a knife."

"But you wanted me to think you were about to."

"That's right," he said. "For the thrill."

"The *thrill?*"

"The thrill of what it's like right before your life ends. What's more sensational than your last breath? It makes your orgasm feel like you're entering the gates of heaven."

These crazy fucking Americans, she thought.

The handsome green-eyed man stood pleading before her, the dagger gripped tightly in his hand, outstretched like an offering to pagan a God.

As the adrenaline slowly subsided, Silvia approached him. He willingly relinquished the dagger, and her lips found his. She pressed the edge of the blade against his cheek, trimming a section of stubble with razor precision. He grinned and kissed her neck, revealing Ellie watching from the doorway.

"You enjoy watching me fuck your husband?" Silvia asked, pressing the blade to George's throat. "Say uh huh, bitch."

Ellie grinned.

Silvia stepped out into the hallway dressed in the bathrobe she'd taken from Ellie and George's suite. As she headed for her room, she heard someone call out to her. She turned to see Jack stepping off the elevator.

"Jack!"

"Nice outfit," he said jokingly as he sized her up.

She took a breath. "Yeah. I just came from the pool. I'm headed back to my room to shower."

"I was hoping to run into you. It's been a hell of a day. Lots to share. If you're free later, maybe we could have dinner?"

Silvia smiled. "I'd love to. A quiet, relaxing evening is just what I need."

"Six o'clock in the dining room?"

"That'd be perfect."

Jack nodded. "It's a date."

Chapter 20
Hit List

On the street corner at the end of the alley, Inspector Righetti lit his cigarette and inhaled as much as his lungs would allow. Leaning back against the side of his vehicle, he watched as the firefighters and police officers milled about in the aftermath. A neighbor, having seen the flames through the window, had called the fire department, saving the rest of the building from crumbling in on itself.

"Bloody-fucking-mess," Gallo said as he approached. "It was his own damn fault, of course." He offered Righetti a sip from his flask, but the Inspector waved it off.

They watched as the man Righetti now knew to be Alberto Marino (cousin of Marco), was zipped into a body bag by the paramedics.

"I suppose he was in on the killings with his cousin. Why else would he react to us the way he did?" Gallo mused as he took a swig.

"He was guilty of something." Righetti took another drag. "Something pretty terrible to get him to set his own fucking home ablaze in order to escape it."

Alberto's body, bagged and tagged, was wheeled past on a gurney and lifted into the back of an ambulance.

"Ride along with them," Righetti said. "I'll catch up with you later today."

"You're sticking around?"

"I'll handle the paperwork. It'll give me time to decompress."

"Whatever you say, Inspector." Gallo hopped inside the ambulance to accompany the corpse. He and Righetti saluted one another before the doors closed, then the ambulance pulled away, its siren wailing.

"Inspector," one of the officers said as he approached. "There's a gentleman here, says he needs to speak with you."

Righetti didn't bother to look, instead keeping his sights on the departing ambulance. "About what?"

"He's from the resort. Said it was extremely urgent and would only share the details directly with you. Someone at the station must have told him you were down here."

Righetti glanced over and saw the weasel-esque concierge from Terme del Paradiso standing with a few of the other officers, a manilla folder clutched in both hands. Exhaling a puff of smoke like a fuming dragon, Righetti told the officer to send the man over. Giddily, the concierge hurried across the street.

"Inspector," he said, releasing one of his hands from the folder to shake. "I'm not sure if you remember me. Giancarlo. I work at Terme del Paradiso." Giancarlo's hand lingered in the air for several seconds, finally retracting once he realized Righetti was not going to shake it.

"Must be something pretty fucking important for you to drive all the way over here," Righetti said.

"Oh, I assure you, it is."

"Let's have it then."

"All right, well, it all—" Giancarlo noticed the singed material of Righetti's jacket. "Are you—"

"You didn't come here to check on my well-being. Say what you came to say."

Flustered, Giancarlo attempted to arrange his thoughts, his eyes drawn to the burns on the Inspector's clothing. Had he been in the fire? What chaos had unfolded here?

Righetti took another drag of his cigarette. "Well?"

As if snapping out of a trance, Giancarlo responded with the rehearsed lines. "Last night, one of the guests called down to reception to make an after-hours appointment at the spa. Silvia Pasquale. When she failed to show up, they rang her room, but there was no answer. Considering what happened to Mrs Gaeta and our two employees, I felt I should go up to her room to check on her. I'm especially paranoid about all of these occurrences, as you can understand. I couldn't get the thought of Mrs Pasquale in peril out of my head. I knocked, but there was no answer. I knocked a few more times, and still nothing, so I entered and announced myself and my intentions of simply doing a wellness check. And there she was in bed, naked and high on some sort of drug, I imagine. She was so disconnected that I don't think she even realized I was there."

"I feel as though you're on the verge of confessing to a crime," Righetti said.

"I assure you there was no ill behavior on my part, Inspector. I am but a good samaritan."

Righetti gestured for Giancarlo to continue his story.

"Seeing clearly why she'd missed her appointment, I was about to leave, but something caught my eye." Giancarlo slid a photograph from the manilla folder and held it up for Righetti to see. "This photograph on the nightstand."

Righetti looked at the four Italian soldiers captured in the picture. "An old war photo?"

Giancarlo flipped it over, revealing the handwritten inscription.

Frezza, Conti, Rossini & Cairo — 1943

"I recognized two of the names immediately. Conti: the surname of our cook who was attacked. And Rossini, which everyone knows to have been Vittoria Gaeta's maiden name."

Righetti took the photograph from Giancarlo, his interest piqued.

"The other two names I don't recognize," Giancarlo said. "Cairo and Frezza."

But Inspector Righetti recognized them both. Cairo, maiden name of Lucia Tranquilli, who, along with her husband and two others, had been brutally murdered a few weeks prior in their family vacation home. And Frezza: the maiden name of Silvia Pasquale, the woman whose room Giancarlo had found the photograph in. Silvia Pasquale, the widow who the American, Jack Ivy, had claimed to be his alibi for when Illaria Conti had been attacked.

"Do you make a habit of stealing things from your guests' rooms?" Righetti asked.

"Certainly not," Giancarlo said with disdain. "I simply felt it necessary to take it to show you, to help prevent any more murders."

"Your resort is full of amateur detectives, isn't it?" Righetti's condescension was palpable.

"Surely it's no coincidence that the names of two of the victims are there. No doubt these men in the photograph are their fathers."

Righetti knew Giancarlo's theory wasn't far-fetched. In fact, it matched the American's theory that the killer was picking the women off as retribution for their fathers' sins. But why did Silvia Pasquale have the photograph with her?

"And Mrs Pasquale doesn't know you have this?"

"As I said, I'm quite sure she's unaware I was in her room at all. Drug addicts aren't the most observant individuals."

"And where is she now?"

"Still at the resort, last I saw. Her reservation is through Thursday. Though this morning we had several guests check-out earlier than planned."

Righetti laughed through his nose, a sound somewhere between a scoff and a snort. "Gotta love the rich. Two vicious attacks is ignorable. But *three*? I guess that exceeds the acceptable limit for these people."

"They are a different breed, aren't they, Inspector?" Giancarlo smiled.

Righetti gave him an obvious judgmental look, examining the man's classy suit and moisturized hands that had never seen a day of hard labor.

"Indeed."

"If you'd like, I can inform Mrs Pasquale you'd like to speak with her, to clear all this up."

Righetti considered the offer. Alerting Silvia Pasquale that she was likely the next target of Marco Marino *would* be the right thing to do. The news would lead her to pack her bags, flee the resort, maybe even Sicily altogether. Righetti knew that's what he should do to ensure her safety.

But Marco was still out there. And with his cousin (and possible accomplice) dead, he'd not be returning home. If Silvia were gone, Marco himself might attempt to escape the country. Vanish never to be seen again. Righetti felt it was almost a certainty. If there were to be any chance of catching him, Silvia would need to remain unaware of the danger.

She'd need to be the bait.

Chapter 21
Blood On The Beach

The dining room was much emptier than it had been earlier in the week. Many of the guests had checked out ahead of schedule, leaving a noticeable vacancy at many of the tables previously reserved for dinner. Those remaining did their best to feign ambivalence, attempting to enjoy the evening in the wake of the attacks. Even the staff, who by trade were experts at acting cheerful, struggled to keep up appearances.

Jack and Silvia sat across from one another, picking at their food, neither fully present. The arrival of the waiter delivering fresh cocktails was enough to make them both aware of their own distant behavior.

"How is it?" Jack asked.

"Same as yours, it seems," Silvia said.

"Mine's fine, actually. I'm just—"

"I know," she said, putting the need for an explanation to rest. "Me too."

Jack couldn't help but relive the moment he found Monica's body in the rose garden.

Pruning shears. Jesus Christ.

Was a knife any more civilized? He wasn't sure. But the image of the shears clipping through the poor woman's neck, severing her windpipe like it was nothing more than overgrown foliage, somehow felt colder, as if lacking the deranged intimacy one would imagine a knife wielding killer to possess.

"I wish I'd been with you... when you found her," Silvia said.

Jack looked at her with surprise. "Why?"

She shrugged. "Sometimes it helps to experience traumatizing things with a partner. So you can share the experience. Heal together. That sort of thing."

"I'm *glad* you weren't there. I wouldn't wish that sight on anyone."

"Things like that, dead bodies brutally maimed, think of how often men in the war would have experienced it. How many times each day? Over and over. And the aftermath. Bullets and bombs. Knives. It's a horror many had to endure for years."

Reading between her words, Jack said. "Your father—"

"Was a soldier, yes."

His worry sank to an even greater depth. "Was he in the Black Brigade?"

Surprised by the accuracy, Silvia paused a moment before answering. "He was. I suppose in his heart he still is. You can alter one's attire, but at their core, they never change."

A dozen devastating scenarios ran through Jack's head. Being the first time he'd spoken with her since she departed to see her father, Jack had yet to tell her everything he'd discovered. The daggers. Marco. Luca's theory.

"Silvia, I think you should leave this place," he said.

"It's probably a good idea for both of us, too. Honestly, I was surprised to see you were still around when we ran into each other in the hallway."

"There's more going on here than you realize. Vittoria's father, and the cook's — they were both in the Black Brigade as well."

"That's no shock. We're all daughters of ruthless men," she said, taking a bite of her dinner. "Ruthless men know how to survive. They know how to keep their families alive."

"Silvia, these attacks — that's why they're happening. They're revenge killings. This man, Marco — he's an employee here — I think he's targeting the children of those responsible for his family's murder."

"His family? How do you know anything about an employee's family?"

"Luca. He told me all about it."

She contemplated Jack's story. "Did you share that with the police?"

"I did. And hopefully they're working on tracking him down."

"And you think I should leave, as not to become his next victim?"

"I don't want to see anything happen to you."

Silvia donned a smile that quickly faded. She raised her glass.

"To better times," she said.

Jack hesitated, worried that his warning had not landed with enough impact, then he clinked his cocktail against hers. "To better times."

They drank.

Silvia leaned back in her seat. "I'd love to say that in all my life I'd never seen so much horror. But it wouldn't be true, would it?"

"Our generation has lived through a lot."

"I imagine all generations feel that way."

Touching the edge of the glass to her lips, Silvia held it there for a moment as a sign of contemplation before drinking. "Come. I need some air."

Jack followed her out to the terrace. Light from the cabana bar below cast a warm glow across the beach, a shimmer of luminosity along the otherwise tenebrous coast. The crowd seemed just as lively as it had the previous night. Music played, people danced, drinks spilled.

"Perhaps we should join them," Silvia said. Jack couldn't tell if she was being serious. If she were, he wasn't sure he could survive the strength it would take to pretend he was enjoying himself. Then again, he didn't feel either of them were providing the best company at the moment.

Trying to steer the topic away from the cabana bar, he said, "I thought I might see you last night, after you returned from visiting your father."

"I wasn't in any state to see you, Jack. Wasn't in any state to see anyone."

Jack immediately regretted saying it. "No need to explain. I wasn't intending to place guilt."

"It's fine," Silvia assured him.

Jack took another drink. "For what my sentiments are worth, I *do* think you should leave the resort. At least until we know the police have the killer in custody."

"And what about you?"

"I'm not really in a position to be adjusting my travel plans, unfortunately."

"But if you could?"

He chuckled. "I'd be long gone. After getting your contact information, of course."

"So you could, what? Come visit me?"

"Yeah, maybe. Would that be permissible?"

She grinned. "Yeah, maybe." She took another sip, savoring the taste. "These are really quite good."

"Luca is quite the artist, isn't he?"

"What am I going to do when I don't have him at my beck and call, I wonder?"

From the terrace, they could see into the lounge. Luca was stirring a cocktail in a metal shaker, snaring the attention of a middle-aged woman who stood leaning over the bar top, intentionally pressing her breasts together to show off her cleavage to the handsome employee.

"Maybe you could hire him to be your personal bartender," Jack said.

"Personal bartender? How much of a lush do you take me for, that I should need a personal bartender, Jack Ivy?"

Jack laughed. "I guess there's plenty of other things more practical to spend one's money on."

"Do you know anyone with a personal bartender?"

"I don't."

"And neither do I. I mean, I know people who have servants, of course. Butlers, maids, that kind of thing. But specifically, a bartender? You'd need to consume a lot of cocktails to justify that."

"I don't think the rich need to justify their expenses. Another reason you should cut your vacation short."

"All right, Jack. I hear you. Another day or two here isn't worth the risk, regardless of how thin your hypothesis may be."

A smile warmed his face. "Better safe than sorry, as they say."

"Now, being so late, it's more practical I check-out in the morning. Maybe I can convince someone to stay the night with me. For protection, of course."

"I'm sure someone would be happy to oblige. For protection."

Silvia leaned in and Jack's arm slid around behind her back, gently pulling her closer. Their lips met and for a moment, Jack let the savagery of the recent events fade from his mind. He wished there was a table nearby to set his cocktail down and free up his other hand so that he could hold Silvia even tighter. Every cell in his body wanted to pick her up and carry her to his room, to relive the thrill of their first night together. He couldn't recall the exact number of times they'd fucked that evening. Was it twice before Silvia ordered up the bottle of red wine from room service? Then once after that? Or was it twice after that? They'd finished the entire bottle of Sangiovese, which somehow managed not to turn his stomach even after all the cocktails that had preceded it. He recalled leaning over in bed to see her at the dinette, staring at her perfect, naked backside as she filled their glasses, meticulously pouring so as not to spill a single drop.

Drinking. Fucking. Sightseeing. It's what vacations were intended for, wasn't it?

As their lips parted, and Jack's eyes softly opened, his gaze found nothing to compete with Silvia's beauty. She kissed him again, but before he could close his eyes, his focus shifted subconsciously to the beach below, where a lone figure strolling across the sand was illuminated by the glow from the cabana bar.

Jack pulled back, startling Silvia with his jarring movement. Reading the concern in his face, she looked over her shoulder in an attempt to see whatever had alarmed him.

"What is it?"

"That man, there on the beach," he said, stepping away from Silvia. "That's him."

"Him, who?"

"Marco. It's him, I'm sure of it."

"Marco? The man you said—"

Jack watched as the man on the beach continued to cross through the patch of light. Even at that distance, Jack recognized him clearly.

"Call the police," Jack said, heading for the spiral staircase that led down to the first level.

"Where are *you* going?" Silvia asked.

He was already halfway down the steps when he answered, "Call them! Tell them Marco Marino is at the resort."

"*Jack!*" Silvia shouted from the top of the staircase behind him.

There was no time to waste. If he didn't keep tabs on Marco, the man would easily slip out of reach again. With any luck, he could keep him at bay until the cops arrived.

Sprinting past the cabana bar toward the beach, Jack felt the eyes of the oblivious guests regard him with brief, annoyed expressions before returning to their festivities. As he stepped off the path, his dress shoes sunk into the sand, betraying his balance. He gathered himself and trudged onward, rounding a shrubbery that blocked his view.

Marco was there, nearing the edge of the light cast by the cabana bar. A few more feet and he'd fall into the velvety blue shadow that existed beyond the resort's glow.

"*Marco Marino!*" Jack shouted.

Marco turned, surprised anyone was so close to him on the otherwise vacant beach. Perplexed, he stared at Jack approaching.

"Just stay right there," Jack said, catching his breath.

The bottle of whisky in Marco's hand rose to his mouth and drained a healthy amount. The striking blue eyes, which Jack had been so taken aback by upon their last meeting, were surrounded in bloodshot red, like tiny sapphire islands in matching seas of gore.

"What do you want, friend?"

The word struck Jack like a sledgehammer. *Friend?*

"The police have been looking for you," Jack said. "There's something they need to discuss."

"About the murders, I imagine."

"Yeah. That's right." Jack wanted to look over his shoulder, to see if anyone had followed him out to the beach, but he dared not take his eyes off Marco, who took another swig from the bottle.

Jack took a step toward him, the soft sand swelling around his shoe. "I think it's best you come back with me to the resort. We can talk there."

"Why would I go anywhere with *you?* I don't even know who the hell you are."

"My name's Jack. I'm... a guest here at the resort."

Marco chuckled. "What the fuck are you talking about, friend?"

There was that word again. *Friend.* Jack could feel his teeth gnashing. The thought of being anything remotely close to friends with the man who murdered Vittoria was enough to make him want to smash Marco's head in.

"They know, Marco. You hear what I'm saying? They know. So, just come with me. Make it easier for everyone. No one else needs to get hurt."

"Hurt? *Hurt?* What the hell do you know about hurt?" Marco pointed the mouth of the bottle at Jack.

"Marco, what happened to your family was—"

"What the fuck did you just say? My family?" Tears welled in his red eyes. "You don't—"

Marco turned away, and Jack thought he was going to keep walking, until he spun back around and in a broken voice shouted, "Do you know how it felt, coming to work every day, knowing her father was responsible for my family's death?"

Jack raised his hands defensively. "Marco, we can—"

"My wife is *dead*. My daughter is *dead*. Maybe I'm happy one of theirs is dead now, too."

This son of a bitch. Jack took another step closer, his anger and confidence growing simultaneously. "Being born the daughter of a fascist doesn't make one guilty of their father's crimes."

Marco used the sleeve of his jacket to wipe the tears from his face. "I've put up with it for as long as I can. No more. I'm done. I'm done with all of it."

He threw the bottle down in front of Jack and it landed softly in the sand, a splash of whisky escaping through the neck.

"The blood just never stops. I kept telling myself to accept it, that it's the only way to survive, but I just can't. Not anymore. I've known Death far too long. No matter where I go, there he is, staring me in the face, reminding me of... everything. Monica tried helping me, tried to keep me sane, and calm, but now she's..."

Jack watched as Marco's hand moved inside his jacket.

"Marco?" he said.

The light from the cabana bar glinted across the blade of the straight razor as Marco withdrew it from his jacket. "Time for me to go, friend."

The crack of the gunshot came from behind Jack, and he felt something whizz past him. A jet of blood popped out of Marco's chest. Screams swarmed the air, and Jack turned to see Righetti standing behind him with his pistol raised like some old Western gunslinger.

Past the Inspector was Silvia, her hands covering her mouth as though to keep from crying out at the sight of Marco, who lay motionless in the sand, the gunshot wound dead center, the straight razor resting beside him.

Chapter 22
Debrief

It was verging on 10pm.

The Inspector's office was feeling like a second home to Jack. The encounter on the beach and the chaos of police and media at the crime scene had left him completely drained of any mental strength. Sitting beside Silvia, across the desk from Inspector Righetti, they waited for Gallo to return with their coffees.

"It's a hell of a thing," Righetti said, crushing out the remnants of his cigarette into the ashtray. "Just a hell of a thing."

Silvia's hand slid to Jack's lap, found his hand, and squeezed. "So you think it was him then, Inspector?"

"Had to be. And his cousin, who we dealt with earlier today, must have been complicit in all of it. Only explanation for him doing what he did, trying to burn us alive and all that. I assume he thought we were coming to arrest the both of them, and knowing they'd been caught, decided to go out in a blaze of glory, so to speak. Jack's theory about Marino wanting revenge for his family's death must have been sound."

A wave of relief fell upon Jack. No longer was he under Inspector Righetti's microscope. No longer was he public enemy number one. So, he could hardly believe it when he let the words slip out.

"As much as I appreciate that, Inspector, I do wish there was more for us to go on. To prove it, I mean."

"You're fucking kidding me, right? Not so convinced all of a sudden?" Righetti asked condescendingly.

Jack was careful how he answered. Of course, he wanted the spotlight off of himself, but he also wanted to make damn sure that the killer, or killers, were indeed laid to rest.

"As an attendant at the resort, Marino had access to room keys. He let himself into Vittoria Gaeta's room and killed her while Elio Gaeta was out cold. Although Vittoria was his first victim at the resort, his initial target had to have been Illaria Conti, the cook. She's the reason he got himself a job there. To get close enough to kill her. Vittoria just fell into his lap when her husband booked their stay," Righetti said.

"And Monica?"

"We believe she was only collateral damage. We looked into her family. Father wasn't in the Black Brigade. They were partisans, just as Marino had been."

"Then why kill her?"

"You said she had seen someone disposing of evidence in the furnace, likely the clothing Marino was wearing when he attacked Illaria Conti. Monica was putting the pieces together, realized he was the killer, and so he knocked her off to keep her quiet. It's why he didn't use one of the daggers to do her in. She wasn't one of his initial targets."

"Christ," Silvia said.

"The one piece I can't quite make fit is why you had this in your room, Mrs Pasquale." Righetti pulled a photograph from his desk. *The* photograph. And slid it across to Silvia. "You recognize it?"

She stared at the photograph with utter confusion, then glared up at Righetti. "How did you get this?"

"That's a *yes*, I take it?"

Jack's eyes bounced back and forth between them, trying to catch up.

"Yes. Of course I recognize it," Silvia said.

"Can you tell me who those men are?" Righetti asked.

"This one's my father," she said, tapping the youthful face of Silvano Frezza. "The others were soldiers in his company."

"Cairo, Rossini and Conti," Righetti said, flipping the photograph to reveal the handwritten inscription on the back.

Conti. Jack felt his hairs stand on end.

Righetti reached across the desk and tapped the photograph. "Conti, the cook's last name. Rossini is Vittoria Gaeta's maiden name. She very publicly and famously denounced her father years ago when her career took off. And shockingly enough, prior to any of the horror at Terme del Paradiso unfolded this week, four people, one whose maiden name was Cairo, were slashed apart in their family vacation home."

Jack stared at the names. *Frezza, Conti, Rossini & Cairo — 1943*

"This photograph is a hit list, Mrs Pasquale. And by all manner of speaking, you're on it. It's evident Marino had targeted the daughters of the four men in this photograph as revenge for the death of his family."

"I know the things my father and other fascists did during the war were atrocious. I won't sit here and defend any of it," she said.

Righetti looked at her with sincerity as he said, "I assure you, the sins of the father will not be passed on to the children. You and the other daughters of the men in that photograph have done nothing deserving of Marino's wrath."

"Christ, you would've been next," Jack said quietly. Silvia looked at him, and he could tell she was thinking back to his warning, urging her to leave the resort.

"In all likelihood, Marino was there tonight to cross the last name off his list. I was keeping an eye on you, Mrs Pasquale. As soon as I saw this photograph, I tailed you, watched you both up there on the terrace, and when Jack here bolted for the beach, I was already close enough to come to his aid."

Righetti spotted Gallo through the blinds, holding a trio of coffees, and waved him inside.

"Grazie," Righetti said, as Gallo passed them out.

Silvia continued to stare at the photograph.

"You're lucky to be alive, miss," Gallo said, gesturing at the photograph. "If that slimy concierge hadn't given that photograph to the Inspector here, who knows what would have—"

Gallo caught the fuming expression on Righetti's face much too late.

"Oh. Hadn't gotten that far, I see," Gallo said sheepishly.

"Concierge?" Silvia asked.

"Giancarlo, from the resort," Gallo added.

"That'll be all, Gallo," Righetti said.

Gallo nodded and backed out of the office. Silvia stared at Righetti, waiting for an answer.

"The concierge, *Giancarlo*," Righetti said the man's name with a thinly veiled disdain, "Found this photograph in your room. He thought it was integral to the investigation into the attacks and delivered it to me."

"When was he in my room?"

"He said he'd gone to check on you when you failed to show up for an after-hours spa appointment."

Silvia sat in silence, and Jack could tell she was processing all the information that had just been thrown at her.

Righetti let her take a moment before he finally asked, "I *am* curious, Mrs Pasquale, why you had this photograph in your possession."

"It's my photograph. Why shouldn't I have it?"

"I'm not questioning your ownership, simply why, of all things one may travel with, you would choose this particular photograph."

"First, I wasn't traveling with it. I only acquired it yesterday afternoon when I went to visit my father at his home outside of Randazzo. That's why I'm out here. To see him."

"And he just happened to give you this specific photograph? One that bares the names of Marco Marino's victims?"

"I asked for it. My mother used to keep it beside her bed when she was alive. It reminds me of her and I wanted to bring it back home with me."

"But you must see how odd this all appears, Mrs Pasquale."

"I agree. Quite odd indeed. Odd that a resort concierge should be allowed to dig through a guest's belongings with impunity. But not so odd, unfortunately, that even after the true murderer is caught, the would-be victim should be made to feel as though she is still at fault."

"That's not what I'm getting at here," Righetti said.

"How things are, and how things should be, are always so far apart," she whispered, shaking her head in disappointment.

Jack thought back to the men catcalling Silvia in the street. She had said the same thing then. *How things are. How things should be.*

"It's my job to investigate all the possibilities," Righetti said.

"Meaning the possibility that I'm the killer, and not Marco? Let me remind you, Inspector, that the night the cook was attacked, Jack and I were together in my hotel room."

"Yes, I recall."

"What then? You think Marino and myself were in cahoots? You said yourself I was likely his next victim. Why work with someone he plans on killing? And what motivation would *I* have to kill those women?"

"I'm merely stating that the existence of a photograph that correlates so clearly with the attacks cannot be ignored."

"Then let me merely state something. You seem to have no idea what is happening and have grabbed onto each branch of information presented to you, assuming you've found the trunk. First Elio Gaeta, then Jack here, then Marino, now me. Where does it end, Inspector? The easiest answer cannot alway be correct. Do your job and actually investigate before you start throwing out accusations."

Silvia stood, nearly knocking her chair over. Jack hesitated, then rose in solidarity with her.

Righetti stared at her, the open blinds separating his office from the rest of the station, Silvia's defiant body language on display for the officers to see. Jack expected him to shout at her, to cast a threat for the way she spoke to him, but the Inspector simply remained in his chair, clenching his teeth.

"Anything else you'd like to say, Mrs Pasquale?"

"I'm quite finished, thank you."

Righetti nodded, his face growing red with restrained rage.

"Then so am I." He jerked his head toward the door, and Jack scooped his arm around Silvia's waist, ushering her out before either she or Righetti could continue the conversation.

Through the station, Jack kept his eyes down. The quicker they were out of there, the better. No need to give anyone an opportunity to continue the unpleasantries.

"Jack!"

He shuddered at the sound of his own name, afraid to turn and see who was calling for him. Was it some officer unsatisfied with the revelation that the foreigner was not to blame for the murders after all?

Hesitantly, he glanced over his shoulder, but as he saw the familiar face of the man approaching him, the tension in his muscles disappeared.

"Luca," Jack said with a smile.

Luca hugged Jack and Silvia simultaneously, both of them surprised by the display of affection. "So very glad the two of you are all right."

"What are you doing here?" Jack asked.

"I came as soon as I heard. *Marco Marino!*" Luca gave Jack a gentle punch in the chest. "What did I tell you?"

Jack nodded, uncomfortable with the level of celebration in Luca's voice over a man being gunned down on the beach. "You were right."

"They say you're the one who found him, yes? That the police wouldn't have been able to put an end to all this without your help." Luca's words elicited a series of contemptuous scowls from the nearby officers.

Jack glanced at Silvia. "Right place, right time, I suppose."

"Modesty. I love it," Luca said, sliding between the two of them. He threw his arms over their shoulders, guiding them toward the exit. "Come. We need to celebrate."

"Luca, I appreciate the offer but it's nearly—"

"Eleven. Yes. The night is young."

"I wouldn't mind a little more time away from the resort," Silvia admitted.

Her vote was all that was needed to sway Jack. "What did you have in mind?"

Luca grinned. "Let me show you the *real* Sicilian nightlife."

Chapter 23
Good News

Illaria was home.

She laid awake in bed, and her sister Valentina, just in from Rome, laid beside her. The night was warm, but Illaria was too afraid to leave the window open. Once again, she couldn't help but feel childish in the face of her fears. What was closing the window really going to prevent? Should her attacker come calling, would the thin pane of glass keep him out?

"Can I get you something? To help you sleep?" Valentina asked.

Illaria rolled over to face her sister. "I'm all right."

"I was going to avoid talking about it more, but I don't think I'm going to be successful in distracting you from it, anyway."

"It's okay. Say what you want to say."

Valentina sat up in the bed. "Do you think it may have been someone you work with... at the resort?"

Illaria, her head still lying restlessly on the pillow, looked up at her sister. "I suppose anything is possible."

"Whoever it was knew you were alone and vulnerable. He knew the details of your shift, maybe even your exact schedule. It's unlikely a random psycho got lucky enough and chose the perfect time to attack you, knowing there'd be no one else in the kitchen."

Illaria pondered the prospect.

The phone rang, and both women jumped. Illaria sat up and reached for the receiver on the nightstand, but Valentina leaned to block her.

"I'll get it," she said protectively.

"I can answer my own phone," Illaria said.

Valentina grabbed the receiver. "Hello?"

Illaria watched intently as her sister conversed with whomever was on the other end of the line.

"Yes, she is, but — May I ask what it is a gentleman would be calling her for at this hour?"

Illaria mouthed the words, *Who is it?*

Valentina held her finger up as she continued her conversation with the Mystery Caller.

"Oh. Oh yes, I see. — I'll let her know. — Luca? Yes, of course. — Thank you."

She set the receiver back down in the cradle and turned to Illaria.

"A friend of yours from the resort. Luca. He said that the police found the killer. Said it was a man who worked with the two of you. Marco Marino."

"Marco?" Illaria could hardly believe it. She'd only met Marco once, but had seen him around the resort several times. He was quiet. Kept to himself mostly. No different from her in that respect.

"He said the police killed him. It's over."

"He's dead?" Illaria asked.

Valentina nodded. "You're safe. It's all over."

Tears of happiness welled in Illaria's eyes. Valentina's arms wrapped around her sister, squeezing her as tight as she could. Illaria winced, both of them having forgotten about her knife wound in all the excitement.

"Oh, my God. Sorry, sorry." Valentina pulled back, both of them laughing. She wiped the tears from Illaria's gleaming eyes.

"I can't believe it," she said, relief sweeping over her, every ounce of fear dissolving immediately.

"So the police actually *are* good for something."

Illaria laughed again, shaking her head at her sister's dark humor. "This is so crazy. I didn't think—"

"I told you it would all be okay."

Illaria slapped her hands around her sister's cheeks. "Thank you. Thank you for coming to be with me. I know it wasn't easy putting everything aside to fly out here."

"You're my sister. How could I not come?"

They hugged again, this time a bit more gently.

"God. Well, if I wasn't fully awake before, I certainly am now." Valentina slid out of bed and pulled on her robe. "Come on. We need to celebrate."

"Valentina, it's the middle of the night."

"And you've got a bottle of wine in the kitchen I've been eyeing. Come on. You dodged death! What better reason to share a drink?"

Illaria nodded. "You're right!"

She jumped out of bed and opened the window, looking out at the Sicilian night sky.

"And I need to hear more about this Luca. He sounded quite handsome over the phone."

Illaria grinned and shook her head. "What does handsome sound like, Valentina?"

"It sounds respectful and confident, I suppose. *Is* he respectful and confident?"

"You can be the judge when you meet him."

"Oh, I'm meeting him now?"

"When he picks me up for our date in a few nights."

Valentina raised her brow in surprise. "A date? I didn't think you had time for dates. I thought you only had time for work. Isn't that what you've always told me?"

Illaria shrugged, her cheeks coloring. "I guess I'm making time."

"Must be special."

"He might be."

Valentina grabbed Illaria's robe off the back of the reading chair and tossed it across the bed to her. "Now I *really* need to hear more."

Chapter 24
The Real Sicilian Nightlife

Luca led Jack and Silvia down the cobblestone street, weaving through the crowd to get to the entrance of the bar he'd told them so much about along the way. The yellow neon sign above the door, which seemed to fizzle, straining to remain lit, welcomed them to Taverna Electric.

Inside, the scene was a raucous crowd, partying, dancing, and drinking beneath a lighting grid that flashed beams of red and blue across the sea of bodies. A band played on the elevated stage, the speakers blaring out their rendition of a British pop song.

As the trio approached the bar, Luca waved to one of the finely dressed bartenders.

"Enzo!" Luca called.

The young bartender, Enzo, smiled brightly upon seeing Luca, leaning over the bar top to greet him with a warm hug.

"Luca! My God, how are you?"

"I'm good. I'm good."

"You're sure? I've heard about all the tragedies at the resort. A psychotic murderer, they say."

"That's all done with now, thankfully. The man's been killed by the police."

Enzo's brow raised with surprise. "The police? Thank the Lord. I thought someone might have to involve the mafia to sort it out."

"I've brought some friends," Luca said, moving aside to reveal Jack and Silvia. "Told them this was the best spot in Taormina."

"You're a good man, Luca. Always bringing people to see me."

"Enzo is the best around," Luca professed to Jack and Silvia. "The resort management has been trying to get him on their payroll for months, but he keeps turning them down."

Enzo laughed. "My friend here embellishes. I'm just a humble bartender."

"That's an utter lie," Luca shot back with a grin. "I've never heard you say a humble thing in your life. At least not with sincerity."

Luca turned back to Jack and Silvia.

"We grew up here together. I know this bastard better than my own brothers." He slapped Enzo on the back and shook him reverently by the shoulder.

"You don't even have brothers," Enzo shouted over the music.

As the two Sicilians laughed, bantering back and forth, Jack noticed Silvia had tuned out the entire conversation. He considered how she must be feeling, knowing that she was almost Marco's next victim. What a sensation, to come so close to death and escape it.

Still, he couldn't help but think of the photograph that Inspector Righetti had produced in his office. Why *did* Silvia have it with her? Could it really have been coincidence? Or was there more to the story that had yet to reveal itself? Either way, now was not the time to discuss it. He could wait to ask her, if it was even his place to ask. Tonight, they needed to do as Luca had suggested: relax, decompress, and celebrate.

"The two of you are staying at the resort?" Enzo asked them.

"Yeah," Jack said.

Silvia nodded.

"And the two of you are... a couple, yes?"

"We only just met a few days ago, actually," Jack said. He smirked at Silvia. "But are certainly enjoying one another's company."

"Very much so," she replied.

"Of course. Of course. That's wonderful," Enzo said. "A little holiday fling. Nothing wrong with that. I see it all the time. Fly in. Fuck around. Fly out. So very easy and so very exciting."

Jack considered how crude Enzo had made it sound. Was that all it was? A holiday fling? He'd had little time to analyze their blossoming romance amidst the horrors, but perhaps the Sicilian was right. In fact, the more Jack thought on it, the more he couldn't help but agree. Of course, that's what it was. How could it be anything more than that? They lived a world apart, after all. In a few more days, Jack would be back in New Jersey, and Silvia still somewhere in Italy. Sure, he could get her contact information, but what was the likelihood he'd actually see her again? He couldn't afford to fly back out here anytime soon, and it would be rather presumptuous of him to imagine she'd travel to the States.

But who knows? Maybe all this tragedy had tied them together in some cosmic manner. Maybe the events of the past few days would engrave themselves into the stone tablet of their lives, making it impossible for them to move on from one another. A love story born of violence and murder.

"It's busier than usual tonight," Luca said.

"Yes, an unexpected group came in. Some high-profile film producer-type and his friends."

"Do you know him? The film producer?" Luca asked Enzo.

"No, never met him. But the guest of honor is rather well known. Especially now. Just released from custody as I understand it. I'm sure the papers will have his name plastered all over the place." Enzo held his hands up as if he were unveiling the headline. "Famous filmmaker no longer suspect in wife's murder."

The pin dropped.

Jack and Silvia exchanged looks. Jack leaned in closer to Enzo, lowering his voice as he said, "Enzo, this filmmaker, you're saying it's Elio Gaeta?"

"Of course," Enzo answered. "Word is his lawyers got him off just a few hours ago. His producer wanted to celebrate him being released. All this publicity will do wonders for his next film's box-office return."

Jack turned to Luca, who was already preparing for damage control. "Jack, listen. Don't let this spoil your night. The two of you need this. Who cares whose party it is? He probably won't even notice you're here. In fact, I doubt if he'll even remember you."

"I find that hard to believe," Jack said.

"You know Elio Gaeta?" Enzo asked.

"We met once. It wasn't pleasant for him."

Silvia's hand found Jack's and their eyes met.

"It'll be fine," she said.

"That's right. It'll be fine, Jack. You two go find a table. I'll get us some drinks," Luca insisted.

Jack scanned the room for Elio as he and Silvia crossed the floor, passing through the sea of guests. A man in a silk scarf vacated a cocktail table and Silvia settled in, pulling Jack along.

"Do you see him anywhere?"

"Just forget about it, Jack."

The singer on stage began belting out a cover of a Siouxsie & The Banshees song, albeit in Italian.

"I don't see him," Jack said.

"Jack." The tone of Silvia's voice forced him to focus on her. "Please. Forget it. Pretend like he's not here, and let's go on with our night."

A woman's giggle cut through the rest of the noise in the tavern. Jack's sights shifted, identifying the swinger couple he'd encountered at the resort pool the day before. They were standing at a table, both of them sloppy drunk, their cocktails spilling over the edge of their glasses as they engaged with another patron.

"Someone's having a good time," Silvia said.

"Yes," Jack said, still staring at the couple.

"You know them?"

Jack took a deep breath. "They propositioned me for a threesome at the resort, actually."

"Oh? And did you accept the proposition?" Silvia asked playfully.

Jack grinned. "No."

"Why not? They're an attractive couple. Too liberal for your taste, Mr Ivy?"

"Would you have accepted?"

Silvia smirked and shrugged. "Maybe."

Luca reached the table with a tray of drinks. He passed Jack and Silvia theirs and the three of them toasted to the end of Marco's terror. He was barely done swallowing when he excitedly shouted across the room.

"Ellie and George!"

He waved at the couple and raised his glass to them. They both waved back with an equal level of excitement.

"Ellie and George?" Jack repeated.

"Have you met them yet?" Luca asked. "They're staying at the resort as well."

"Jack was just telling me about his encounter, as a matter of fact," Silvia said.

"Get you up to their room, did they?" Luca nudged him.

"Why would you think I went to their room?"

"I just assumed by Silvia's use of the word 'encounter' that they invited you for some recreational activities."

"So you're aware they're swingers," Jack said.

Luca took a sip. "Of course."

"Have they invited *you* to their room for recreational activities, Luca?" Silvia asked, raising her brow.

Luca sipped again. "Of course."

"And you accepted?"

"Of course." He gestured at the couple with his glass. "Look at them. They're gorgeous. Don't tell me you turned them down."

"A ménage à trois is a bit too extreme for Jack here."

Luca shook his head disapprovingly. "You Americans. I'll never understand you."

Jack shrugged. "I've taken too many implicating photos of people who didn't want their photos taken to put myself in that situation. It's not because I'm American. It's because I'm—"

"Jack. Jack. I'm only playing with you. Relax. How do you like your drink?" Luca nuzzled the cocktail towards Jack's lips.

They drank, and the music grew livelier with each song. Silvia asked Jack to accompany her to the dance floor, but he declined, admitting his incompetent dancing skills. Refusing to let him spoil her fun, Silvia dragged Luca out instead.

Watching from the sidelines, Jack couldn't help but stare as Silvia grooved to the British pop covers. With every bend, every spin, her movements captivated him. The lights flashed across her skin, red and blue beams crossing randomly into purple as they cut through the dark sections of the room.

A cocktail waitress delivering a fresh tray of drinks to the table interrupted his gaze. He picked up his new glass and wet his tongue. After a few songs, Luca and Silvia retreated to the table, out of breath and laughing, both of them immediately snagging their new beverages.

"I can barely keep up with this one," Luca said, gesturing at Silvia. "You were wise not to let her take you out there, Jack."

They toasted once again.

"So much horror in this world. I find comfort in the company of others." Luca pat Jack on the back.

"Your company has been very comforting during all this, to be sure, Luca," Jack admitted.

"Sometimes you just need that support, yes?" He drank. "You know my friend, Illaria, the cook who was attacked, her sister's out here now. Came all the way from Rome to be with her. Family supporting family. You love to see it."

"I'm sure she'll be relieved to hear about Marino," Silvia said.

"To know the man that's been hunting you has been stopped? What better feeling is there? You yourself know first-hand."

"We're lucky to be alive. All thanks to the two of you passing along your suspicions about Marino. Who knows how long it would have taken the police to catch him otherwise?" She squeezed Jack's arm and kissed his cheek.

Luca finished his cocktail in a final gulp. "Not condoning Marco's actions, of course, but the entire ordeal can really be blamed on the fascists. I mean, you don't get a man like Marco, so clearly mentally and emotionally damaged by the loss of his family, without the horrible actions of the fascist regime. Those loyalist bastards were nothing but blood hungry murderers, killing out of enjoyment. To hell with anyone who still supports that ideology. Their actions will have long-lasting effects on our people, more than we can even begin to comprehend. They damaged this country for decades to come. The best we can do is continue to support change, support growth, and back the leftists at every turn." He turned directly to Silvia. "I have some good literature, if you're ever interested," he said.

"Another night, perhaps."

"We could always use another activist to join the cause." He put his hand on her shoulder as dramatic punctuation, but also to help steady himself as the drinks continued to kick in.

"More drinks," Silvia said, pulling away and heading for the bar.

Jack and Luca watched her go.

"She's a beautiful woman, Jack. And in my experience, it's quite unusual to see such a beautiful woman traveling alone. Those who do, do so because they are either in search of great love, or because they have lost that very thing."

Jack pondered the notion.

"What else is there other than love? What stronger passion exists?" Luca asked, the alcohol soaking his profundity.

What is stronger than love, Jack thought. *What could be a stronger drive for an individual? Something of such passionate vigor. The only thing that could compete would be—*

The sight of Elio Gaeta stole the thoughts from Jack's head. The film-maker was at the bar, a glass of red wine in-hand. As if he could sense Jack's gaze, he turned to him, his brow furrowing as though he were trying to deduce where he knew him from. Then, like a lightbulb flaring on, the memory arrived.

"Oh, Christ," Jack said.

It took Luca a moment to realize what was transpiring.

"What is it?"

"I've found the guest of honor." Jack nodded at Elio.

Luca finally spotted him as Elio turned his back to them.

"Well, at least he's not in a confrontational mood," Luca said.

Silvia returned with their drinks, set them down on the table, and immediately pulled Luca back out onto the dance floor.

Jack could feel the alcohol overwhelming his senses. His eyes bounced between Elio at the bar, Silvia in Luca's arms, and the band rocking out on stage, their music filling the room with swelling volume. As if submitting to some taboo urge, Jack glanced back over at the swinger couple. The woman was staring at him, the rim of her glass pressed coyly to her lips.

What had Luca said her name was? Ellie?

She took a step in his direction and Jack immediately began contemplating the most effective way to turn down her inevitable advances without making a scene. But as her yellow go-go boots hit the dance floor, she changed direction and joined Silvia and Luca. Ellie's arms draped around Silvia's neck. Silvia reached back, pulling Luca in closer, sandwiching herself between the two parties. Hips gyrated in sync with the percussion. Fingertips spidered with each bass twang.

Jack couldn't place the song.

Cilla Black?

Sandie Shaw?

He watched as Ellie's lips whispered into Silvia's ear. Then they closed sensually around her lobe, sucking ever so slightly.

The vocalist cried out in an almost orgasmic croon that crescendoed in a wild scream, and as the song ended, Luca seized the opportunity to exit the dance floor to catch his breath, leaving Silvia behind with Ellie.

"You better be careful," he said to Jack, wiping the sweat from his brow. "I think she's interested in Silvia there. The girl might steal your date away."

Jack nodded. "She just might."

"Unless, of course, you'd consider couple swapping. Ellie and George might float that idea past you again."

"Silvia and I aren't—"

"Yes, yes. I know." Luca picked up his glass, spilling half of it as he tried to direct it toward his mouth.

Jack helped steady him.

"Either way, you're a lucky man," Luca slurred. "And you know, I'm quite lucky as well. Illaria. I'm taking her out on a date. As soon as she's feeling up for it. Malfatti's."

Jack could tell by the way Luca lit up at the topic of Illaria that she truly enraptured the man. Jack smiled, content to hear that his newfound friend was happy.

"That's great, Luca," he said with sincerity. "I'm sure the two of you will enjoy yourselves."

"She's quite the woman. Dedicated to her craft. She may even become a chef one day. Wouldn't that be something?"

"I hope she does."

Luca nodded. "Yeah. Yeah."

Jack looked at him, unsure how long the man's legs would support his swaying top half.

"You okay, Luca?"

"Am I okay?" Luca laughed. "I'm really quite drunk, I think. So, yes. I'm wonderful. I appreciate you asking."

"Maybe we should call it a night?"

Luca's hand clasped around the back of Jack's neck and he steered him to face the dance floor. "You see your woman out there? Does she look like she's ready to call it a night?"

Silvia was brimming, dancing as though all the worries of the world had melted away. How could Jack disrupt such a moment?

"But you're right about me. Time to be heading off." Luca pat him on the chest. "Just don't be leaving her out here alone, Jack."

"Wouldn't dream of it."

"I'll see you tomorrow, of course." Luca tipped an invisible hat and sauntered toward the exit.

"I'm sure we'll be needing a bit of the hair of the dog," Jack said, half to himself. Luca waved to him, shouldered the door open, and disappeared outside.

Jack flagged down a passing cocktail waitress.

"Restroom?"

She pointed toward the back of the tavern.

"Grazie," Jack said in his best Italian.

He headed through the crowd and pushed the restroom door open. As it closed behind him, the sound of the band was reduced to a muffled hum. He relieved himself, washed his hands, and took a deep breath before venturing back out into the heart of the tavern.

Maybe he'd take a turn on the dance floor with Silvia, after all. Why the hell not? He didn't know anyone in Sicily, so there was no one there he had to fear judging his lack of dance skills.

In the short time he had been in the restroom, another group had commandeered the table they had been occupying since they arrived. A trio of black clad poet-types in mesh tops.

He approached the dance floor, expecting to see Silvia still swaying in the sea of neon lights, but she was nowhere in sight. He scanned the crowd. No Silvia. He looked toward the bar. No Silvia.

Ellie emerged from the dance floor and returned to her own table, frantically guzzling a glass of water beside her husband.

What did Luca say his name was?

George.

Jack approached them, asking Ellie if she knew where Silvia had gone.

"Hey, I remember you!" George clapped with inebriated excitement.

"I'm looking for my friend," Jack said to Ellie. "You were dancing with her out there just a few minutes ago."

"You're the guy from the pool," George proclaimed.

"Yeah. Listen—"

"We were really disappointed when you turned us down, you know? But hey, there's always tonight!" George squeezed Jack's shoulder.

Jack ignored George, trying to get Ellie to focus on what he was asking. "My friend. Did you see where she went?"

"Is she not still out there?" Ellie looked over at the dance floor.

"No. No, she's not there."

"I don't know. Maybe the restroom?"

Jack looked back to where he'd just come from.

Of course. She was probably just in the restroom. He felt silly for having panicked. But when he looked back toward the bar again, his panic resurfaced. Elio Gaeta was gone as well. He couldn't risk chalking it up to coincidence.

"This is going to sound strange," Jack said to Ellie. "But do you think you could go into the women's room and check for me?"

"What?"

"I know how that sounds, but I really need to be sure she's okay. Can you just check for me?"

Ellie looked at George, who shrugged.

"I guess so," she said reluctantly.

"Thank you. They're right over there."

"Yeah, I know."

Ellie slid past him and Jack watched her weave through the crowd and enter the women's restroom. He waited impatiently, all the while George smiling at him from an uncomfortable proximity. Finally, the door to the women's restroom opened again and Ellie returned.

"She's not in there," she said, taking another drink of her water.

"You're sure?"

"Yeah. I'm sure. I checked all the stalls."

George leaned in toward Jack. "Looks like she abandoned you, fella. So what do you say we—"

But Jack was already on the move. He hurried to the bar and waved Enzo over.

"Hey! How's it going?" Enzo asked. "I saw Luca—"

"Elio Gaeta," Jack said, cutting him off. "Did you see where he went?"

Enzo chuckled. "I thought you were gonna steer clear of that guy."

"*Where did he go?*" Jack shouted.

Enzo took a step away, taken aback by the hostility in Jack's voice. Pointing to the door, he answered, "He left."

Jack bolted for the exit.

Throwing open the door, he let the tunes from the band escape into the night for only a moment before they were sealed back inside the tavern. The cobblestone street was pristinely lit, a combination of sea mist blown in from the bay, and the warm hue of the streetlamp positioned perfectly along the curb just outside the entrance. Looking like some harbinger of death, Elio Gaeta stood on the corner, taking a long drag of his cigarette.

He regarded Jack. "I suppose you're looking for that woman you were with? The one from the resort?"

Jack was hesitant to engage, yet eager to find where Silvia had gone. He kept his response brief.

"I am."

The cherry flared at the tip of Elio's cigarette. "I remember you, you know. You're the one from the lounge that night. *Black Sunday? Marnie?* You're quite the comedian."

There was no reason to take the bait. Any further conversation to explain away his actions that evening would be pointless.

"The woman I was with—"

"Hard to mistake that one. Beautiful." He took another long drag, the cigarette smoldering at a rapid pace. "Like my wife was."

The tension between the two men was palpable. Jack knew Elio was hoping he'd say more. Ask more. And Jack *wanted* to say more to Elio. Maybe even say something about Vittoria. How Elio had so clearly mistreated her. How he'd reduced her to an accessory, a showpiece to exemplify his notoriety as a second-rate filmmaker. But it wasn't the place. And with Silvia suddenly missing, neither was it the time.

"They tell me you were with her that night. My wife. Vittoria. After I passed out."

Jack's first inclination was to lie, but the fire in his chest — maybe bolstered by the scotch — gave him the vigor to admit his transgressions.

"That's right."

Elio grinned. "Proud of that, are you?"

"She was quite a woman. And I'm deeply sorry for what happened to her. Maybe if you'd not drank yourself into a stupor, you could have prevented it."

"You know, we were quite in love for a time, she and I. I'm not sure when that faded. It happens gradually without you realizing it, I think. And then so much time passes that there seems to be no rhyme or reason to it, and you can't explain the why of it all. The passion just... ends. And each of you has somehow diverged onto separate paths without even noticing. At least, that's what I tell myself. Though something tells me *my* experience was singular. I think maybe Vittoria knew it was happening in real time. She was always more keen than I."

He threw down his cigarette butt and stamped it out before reaching into the breast pocket of his jacket for a flask adorned with a painted rendition of Elsa Lanchester. Unscrewing the lid, he took a swig.

"Willful ignorance on my part. Is that what they call it?"

Jack couldn't contain himself any longer. "Maybe if you didn't treat her like—"

"Like what? A goddamned goddess? I made that woman's career. She was a runway model. I turned her into a fucking movie star. I put her on the map. Put her on a silver platter for the masses to consume. And consume they fucking did. Ate her right up. Vittoria Gaeta. Movie. Fucking. Star. Oh, but as soon as I don't give her the lead role in my next picture, as soon as I don't develop a standard for nepotism, I'm cast as the villain?"

Jack cut into Elio's inebriated tirade. "I don't know anything about—"

"No, of course you don't. You just pretended to be a fan of my films to mock me. And then you, what? Drugged me so you could fuck my wife?"

"Drugged you? I don't—"

"Please. I'm a filmmaker — a functioning alcoholic. A night of cocktails isn't going to put me out so hard that I can't hear my wife being murdered ten feet away. You drugged me. You and your bartender friend."

The notion bled through Jack's mind.

"You think I don't know? I heard all those loudmouth police officers discussing their theories while I was in Righetti's jail cell."

"Listen. What happened that night—"

"Such a beautiful young woman, tired of her husband, ready to jump on the first charming American cock that perked up in her direction."

Jack turned to exit the conversation, but Elio grabbed him firmly by the forearm. Their eyes met, jaws clenching in defiance of one another.

"I want to hear it," Elio said. "I want to hear how you fucked her. I want to hear each and every position you put her in. I want you to do that for me, because I'd rather think of her last moments of pleasure than of the final breaths of agonizing torture she endured at the hands of that psychopath Marino."

It was clear from the pain in Elio's eyes that he had no malice within him. Wherever Silvia had run off to, this man had nothing to do with it.

"She was happy," Jack admitted. "I'm not sure what else to say other than that. Yes, we slept together. I enjoyed it. And I would feel confident in saying she did, too. And afterwards she left my room and went back to yours. I'll admit, I assumed, as most did, that you were the one that killed her."

Elio seemed ashamed by the tears welling in his own eyes.

"I could never hurt her," he said, chuckling with acceptance. "Not physically, anyway. Though I see I may have very well been the villain of her story."

He pulled out his pack of cigarettes and lit another.

"The woman I was with tonight. Where did she go?" Jack asked.

Elio pointed down the dark alleyway beyond the tavern.

"She headed that way. Toward the docks."

Jack turned to face the shadowy, narrow passage.

"You better go after her," Elio said. "It's not safe for a woman to be out alone this late at night."

Chapter 25
Run Amuck!

The further Luca strolled down the alleyway, the more potent the smell of the sea became. He could hear the waves crashing, battering boats in the harbor. Though he'd intended to head home when he left the tavern, the alcohol had left him feeling too drunk to attempt the long walk back. He'd seen men stumble and crack their heads open after too many glasses of wine, and with everything he'd consumed, there was no sense in taking the risk.

The beach will be my bed for tonight, he thought.

He'd find a nice spot, somewhere soft in the sand, a safe distance from the rising tide. The resort management wouldn't be happy with him failing to show up for his shift, but after all the terrible incidents that had occurred, he was confident they couldn't hold it against him for too long. Besides, there was no possibility of him sobering up in time, and if they saw him in such a state, they'd send him home anyway.

It had been a few years since he had felt this drunk. And even then, it hadn't been quite this severe. His head was swimming. His vision blurring.

Enzo makes one hell of a cocktail.

A dog, its fur shaggy and matted, greeted him. Luca let it lick his palm, apologizing that he had nothing to share. The dog circled him a few times, hoping some hidden treat would reveal itself.

"Next time, boy."

The dog whined, then took off down the coast.

"I wouldn't mind the company," Luca shouted.

The beach was vacant. All the boats in the harbor put to rest for the night. He could see only a lone fishing vessel trawling a mile or so out. A light on its bow blinked every few seconds, a gentle repetition that felt as calming to Luca as counting sheep. The thought of such a seafaring life reminded him of what could have been had he not secured his job at Terme del Paradiso. He would often tell others it had been the best decision of his life to apply. A steady paycheck, endless booze at his disposal, and an all-around enjoyable group of locals to work with. Sure, the clientele could get uppity, but by God, did they know how to have a good time.

The trawler's light was suddenly gone. Luca squinted, trying to locate it again. What he initially took for sea mist rolling in, he soon realized was his own vision growing hazier. It was as if he were standing in the middle of a dense fog, no longer able to see clearly.

This isn't the alcohol.

His legs grew weak, his body beginning to sway. He knelt down to keep from falling, then gently lowered himself onto his back. Soft footsteps in the sand from behind him preceded a familiar voice.

"One too many drinks, Luca?"

He rolled over onto his side and forced himself back up to his knees. Struggling to see through his disorientation, he dusted the sand from his palms, then rubbed at his eyes.

"What are you..."

"Easy now," the voice said, and Luca felt a hand settle onto his shoulder.

"I can't... I can't keep my eyes open," he slurred.

"I know. I know." The hand patted him, accompanying the condescending words. "You remind me a lot of my husband. Did I mention that? He too thought the fascists were the worst thing to ever happen to this country. I used to listen to him drone on and on about the evils of

Mussolini, how generations would feel the effects of that man's deeds. *Back the leftists*, he would say. *Back them at every turn*. And I would just sit there, a faux smile plastered across my face, nodding as though the regurgitated sentiments spewing from his mouth were anything but lunacy. How any man that had yet to fight for his country could feel entitled enough to judge those who did, I will never understand."

The hand slid from his shoulder and gathered up the collar of his shirt, twisting it and pulling him upward as though he'd just been secured to a meat hook.

"Why marry a man whose political affiliations I so disdained, you're wondering? Being the daughter of a soldier afforded me very few means of getting by in this world, and certainly not enough to secure the resources I needed to undertake what I'd dreamt of doing since I was a child. Money. The man I married had plenty of it, which meant I had access to everything necessary. It helped me find them. All of them. And as soon as I figured out the perfect way to make his passing look like an accident, I was free to embark on my mission."

Luca felt a sharp pain in his chest, unlike anything he'd ever experienced before. He tried to scream, but the only sound that escaped his mouth was a quiet wheeze. His mouth bobbed open then shut, like a fish gasping for air. Another sharp pain sent his synapses firing like an execution squad. He reached up at the dark figure that stood over him, but as the blade continued to stab into his torso, his arms lost their strength and sagged down to his sides. The wet squelching of battered flesh competed with the crashing waves, and he saw his blood spray out across the woman's white dress.

Even as his head slunk limply to the side, the stabbing did not cease. His sights settled on the bay, somehow accepting his inevitable demise, content at least with his final view. The trawler had reappeared, its blinking light ready to put Luca to rest.

～

JACK STOPPED in his tracks as the horrific sight came into view. Luca was on his knees, his back arched, arms limp. A dark figure stood over him, holding his shirt collar with one hand, while the other repeatedly stabbed a long-bladed knife into his chest.

"Luca!" Jack shouted.

The spotlight from a fishing vessel in the bay clicked on, illuminating the beach and revealing the shadowy figure.

Jack couldn't believe his eyes.

"Silvia?"

Silvia swung the knife once more, slashing open Luca's throat. She released his collar, letting his limp body crumple to the ground. Squaring off, she stared at Jack, the knife in her hand, her dress bathed in wet crimson. Blood dripped from the blade, pattering Luca's motionless chest like rain against a café awning.

Then she ran.

And Jack gave chase.

He was unsure what he'd do if he caught up to her. He was unsure of everything at the moment.

"*Stop!*" he shouted, trailing after her across the wet stone of the harbor. He mirrored her movements, veering down an alleyway, dodging an avalanche of wooden crates that she sent crashing toward him.

Silvia turned a corner, and he followed her out alongside a brick building facing the bay. The rising tide was spreading across the beach, erasing the sand. Waves dashed against the ships in the harbor, jostling them about, threatening to unspool the ropes that anchored them.

Silvia scaled the rickety fire escape stairwell of the building, ascending feverishly toward the top.

"*Silvia! Stop!*"

Jack pursued her up the stairs, the railing shaking violently as he propelled himself forward. She disappeared onto the roof, and as he reached the summit, he advanced cautiously. Moonlight glinted off a wicked-looking blade as it sliced through the air inches from his face. He stepped back, and Silvia slashed again, this time cutting through the lapel of his suit jacket. Her knee struck Jack's gut, and the blade sunk into his left shoulder. He felt the metal scrape against bone and in a moment of primal rage; he grabbed Silvia by the throat and slammed her down on the rooftop.

As she lay there, catching her breath, Jack begged internally for a way to comprehend the situation. What the hell was happening? What had possessed Silvia to murder Luca? It didn't make sense.

He paced in front of her as she sat up.

And he saw the knife in her hand. Saw it clearly. A military blade, cruciform, eight inches in length. It had a curved pommel similar to a pistol, with a cross guard decorated with ball finials.

A Blackshirt's dagger.

"Oh, Christ." Jack ran his hand through his hair, still pacing like an anxious dog. "It was *you?*"

Silvia rose slowly, allowing Jack to distance himself.

"I don't want to hurt you, Jack."

"Why? Why did you do it? Why did you kill those women?"

Silvia turned her back to him, staring out at the city beyond. The view was arguably even better than the one in Jack's room at the resort. From the two-story height of the roof, he could see the architecture of Taormina spread across the horizon.

"Sometimes men think they want answers to questions, then regret it after getting them," she said.

"Why, Silvia?"

"They all deserved what they got."

"Deserved what they got? What could they have possibly done to deserve what they got?"

She turned to face him again, and the haunting look in her eyes caused him to take a step back... a step closer to the edge of the roof. He looked down. Below were the fire escape stairs, and past them, the sandy beach, the moonlit waves lapping against it.

"Silvia. You need to come with me. Put down the knife and come with me."

"Come with you where, Jack? To the police?" She laughed through her nose. "No, I'm afraid I'm not quite done with all I have to do."

She charged forward, startling Jack enough to make him take another step back. The roof vanished from beneath his feet and he tumbled backward through the air. His spine hit the staircase handrail, and he heard an earsplitting crack. The weight of his upper body pulled him downward, and he flipped heels over head and landed flat on his back in the sand.

Staring up at the stars above, what should have been a serene sight was overwhelmed by the realization that all feeling in his body had gone. He knew instantly that the loud crack he had heard was his spine shattering.

Help me!

Help me! Someone, please!

It took him a moment to realize that he wasn't speaking. His cries for help could not escape his head. He attempted to sit up, attempted to roll over onto his side, but no matter how hard he tried, no matter how angrily he screamed at his body to do so, Jack Ivy could not move.

His arms couldn't move. His legs couldn't move.

It was only his eyes, frantically darting from side to side as the horrific reality saturated his mind.

Get up, Jack, he told himself.

Get up, Goddamn it!

Get up!

Get up!

Though he couldn't feel it, the edge of a wave caressed the top of his head, the foamy fringe splashing up just enough to reach his eyes, reminding Jack that high tide was quickly approaching.

Get up, Jack!

Fucking move your ass, or you're going to drown!

Another wave splashed against him.

He heard the clanging of the footsteps slowly coming down the metal staircase.

Get up, Jack!

Get up, Jack!

Get up, Goddamn it!

Chapter 26
High Tide

Silvia stared down at Jack. His body was motionless in the sand, the very edge of the waves kissing the crown of his head. Nothing moved but his eyes, flicking about anxiously, trying to make sense of his predicament. She could see the fear swelling in his pupils as he realized he was paralyzed.

"Oh, Jack. I'm sorry you got yourself tangled up in all this. But no one, especially not some handsome photographer I just met, is going to stop me from what I came here to do. Those women, the ones whose fathers are in the photograph with mine, they weren't targeted for their fathers' sins as you had assumed. They were targeted for betraying their legacies, spitting in the face of all that their fathers had done, all they had fought for. When I was a child sitting on my mother's lap, asking why my father and his friends were such sad men, she told me that their country had turned against them. And to be shunned by your own country is a very painful thing to endure. But sometimes even family members turn on men, and that, that is the most painful of all. Those women, Vittoria, Lucia Cairo, and the Conti sisters, they betrayed their fathers. And *that* I could not allow to go unpunished.

For me, it all started with Vittoria. She denounced her father to the press when her career began to take off. She couldn't risk letting his history of protecting his own country tarnish her modeling career. For Heaven's sake, no. I knew when I read that interview, I had no other choice but to avenge that brave soldier's name. I had to kill her, the way she killed the true story of his sacrifice. I began following her, monitoring her movements, plotting the perfect time to strike.

At the same time, I looked into the daughters of my father's other close friends, Fabio Cairo and Oreste Conti. Cairo's daughter, Lucia, had become an activist in her own right, working for a leftist organization and spouting their ideologies. Illaria and Valentina Conti were raised by their grandfather, an anti-fascist who had never supported his son. He raised them to hate their father and his views after poor Oreste killed himself. All four of them, ungrateful daughters, embarrassments to their family histories, should have been ashamed of what they'd chosen to become. But they were all living their lives as though they had some magical immunity to the past. Like they'd risen to a higher state of being, lifted themselves up on marble pedestals to look down on daddy's disappointing acts.

When I discovered Vittoria's plans to accompany her husband on vacation to Terme del Paradiso, it felt like the stars had aligned, paving the path for me to not only strike down one ungrateful daughter, but all the vile daughters of my father's best friends. I knew that Illaria Conti was working at the resort, and Lucia Cairo's annual beach house visit was planned to occur only a few weeks earlier in Taormina. It could be a single stone's throw, resulting in multiple dead birds.

I started with Lucia. Then on the first night of my stay at the resort I slipped one of my sleeping pills into Elio Gaeta's drink while he was in the lounge. I snuck into his hotel room with a key that I swiped off a maid and waited for Vittoria to return from her fuck session in your room. I donned Elio's signature black hat and raincoat, and ended that little bitch's life, leaving the Blackshirt's dagger as a message, a tribute to her father. The next night, when you and I were together, I drugged your glass of wine, buying me enough time to go down to the kitchen, again dressed in Elio's garb, where I intended to kill Illaria. But she was more skilled than I gave her credit for and I was forced to flee.

Luckily for me, that proved only to help with the grand scheme of things. Letting Illaria survive that night brought her sister, Valentina, all the way from Rome, to check on her. All the daughters in the same place at the same time.

The maid, Monica, she saw me burning Elio's hat and raincoat in the furnace, so I had no other option but to eliminate her. I hated to do it, but I couldn't risk being found out before I'd had time to finish off Illaria.

And poor Luca, you're wondering? Well, you heard all that degrading shit he was spewing in there. That son of a bitch is no better than any of the daughters with his leftist views. What a powerful man he was, with his empty words regurgitated from bastard politicians, and his soft hands that have never seen a hard day's work in his life. Men standing behind a counter slinging drinks don't make history. It's made by the sheer will and determination of those ready and willing to fight for their cause. I simply couldn't help but cut his throat to shut him up for good.

But you, Jack? You, I do have some sympathy for. You're just a fish out of water, flapping upon a shoreline that you couldn't have known would be your demise. I hope you're not in any pain right now. I hope it's all gone numb and you can just rest until it's over. Close your eyes. In a matter of minutes, the tide will rise over your head and you'll be submerged in the comfort of the sea. Find solace in these last few moments that there is nothing you can do to prevent it, so there is nothing you *need* do but relax. Just enjoy the view you have, staring up at this beautiful Sicilian night sky, so gorgeous that I wonder if Heaven itself will look much different. You'll have that answer yourself soon enough. Arrivederci, my friend."

Silvia turned her back to Jack, the tide rising around his cheeks with every surge. She didn't want to watch as the water covered his eyes, then his nostrils, then his mouth. She didn't want to see him swallowed up, slowly drowned, like a helpless kitten trapped in a bag cast out to a watery grave. It wasn't his fault, after all. He hadn't come there to get in her way. But that pesky curious nature of his had done just that. And now he was paying the price.

In another life, perhaps, she thought.

But there was no room for romance in this one. No chance to start anew. She existed for a single purpose now. To avenge her father's friends. To kill the daughters of those sad, forgotten men. And there were still two names left on her list.

Chapter 27
All The Colors Of The Sea

Jack tried to blink the salty water from his eyes as the wave crossed his brow. The next surge crashed over his entire head, and he held his breath until it withdrew. The lingering grit of sand clung to his cheeks until the sea's next stretch came and collected the particles once more. With each wave, the water receded less, until finally Jack's face was swallowed by the surf. He held his breath.

He had never felt fear like this.

Never experienced such extraordinary panic.

And there was nothing he could do. The surface was only inches above his nose, yet he could not make himself sit up to reach it.

After forty-five seconds, he could feel the heat building in his lungs. His temples throbbed. After another thirty seconds, his chest felt like it was going to explode. The urge to breathe was overwhelming — every cell in his body telling him to fill his lungs with the oxygen he knew wasn't accessible. Then, like a dam breaking, his trachea relented, and the sea flooded into his body. The feeling was unbearable. A burning sensation cascaded through his lungs as if his organs were being seared over a stovetop.

Then the pain stopped. And Jack faded from consciousness.

Chapter 28
The Bloodstained Guest

Illaria sat cross-legged on the couch in her living room, as Valentina refilled her wineglass.

"How's Paul?"

Illaria instantly regretted asking, as it was clear the mere mention of Valentina's husband was enough to taint her sister's mood. Valentina refilled her own glass and settled down on the opposite end of the couch. Tucking her legs beneath her, she mirrored her sisters's pose. She ran her fingers across the wallpaper patterned in shades of burnt orange.

"Family is supposed to mean so much," she said. "We're supposed to ignore all their shortcomings, transgressions, and stand by them no matter what."

"Are we?" Illaria asked. "Grandfather didn't believe that."

Valentina took a drink of her wine. "No. I suppose he didn't."

"Sometimes there's nothing you can do to convince someone to maintain their morality. Sometimes people get lost in a sea of confusion and just allow themselves to be taken out further and further with each swell of the wave. And once they realize they've made a mistake, and there is no way for them to swim back without being thrown a life preserver and admitting they were in the wrong — maybe that they've been deceived, duped, brainwashed by someone they thought was going to save them..."

"Are we talking about Paul? Or our father?"

Illaria knew that talk of their father was always a sure way to ruin a nice evening. She wanted to say what she meant. She wanted to say that their father thought Mussolini was the great savior. That he believed Mussolini would bring Italy out of the gutters and into its rightful place in the world. And when it became abundantly clear that the horse he'd placed his bets on was lame, he just couldn't bear to admit he'd made a mistake. So he doubled down. He went even harder, committing himself to the dictator's cause, and hoping beyond hope that somehow he'd emerge victorious and he wouldn't have to say those three simple words.

I was wrong.

But he *was* wrong. Mussolini was never the great man their father thought he was. And even in the end, instead of admitting his shortcomings, admitting his moral failures, their father chose instead to swallow a bullet.

Illaria wanted to say all of that, even though she knew her sister understood the truth just as clearly as she did. But instead, she took a drink.

"And what have you told your friend Luca of our upbringing?"

"He's Italian, Valentina. He understands. The way all Italian men understand."

"Meaning what?"

"Meaning he is the son of a war era father himself. Meaning this history of ours is not unique."

"You think Grandfather would have approved of him?"

"No."

Valentina raised her brow, surprised by the quick response. "No?"

"No. I think he'd be suspicious of him."

"Why's that?"

"Because you should always be suspicious of handsome men."

They laughed. And they drank. And when the bottle was finished, they retired to the bedroom.

"I need to wash my face, but honestly, I just want to pass out," Valentina said.

"I'm not going to pressure you into adhering to your nightly routine, if that's what you're expecting."

Valentina threw a sock at the back of Illaria's head. Without hesitation, Illaria immediately balled it up and threw it back in her sister's face.

"I need to pee," Illaria said, and strolled into the bathroom, closing the door behind her.

Valentina removed her robe and rested it on the back of the chair. Observing herself in the standing mirror, she turned from side to side, analyzing the details of the powder blue pajamas she wore. She'd received them as a Christmas gift from her husband, Paul, a year prior and they made her mind drift to him once more.

The sound of the toilet flushing beyond the closed door preceded the creak of the sink faucet twisting on.

"Just going to wash my face," Illaria called out over the sound of the running water.

Through the open window, a breeze arrived, blowing a wisp of Valentina's hair across her shoulder. Then a gloved hand wrapped around her mouth from behind and she felt an agonizing pain shoot through her body as something blunt slammed down atop the crown of her skull. She wanted to scream for help, but the impact had put her in a daze. Someone shoved her down on the bed, rolling her to her back and covering her mouth once again.

A woman, her dress sticky with a browning crimson paste, straddled atop her. She leaned down close so that her lips were inches from Valentina's face.

"You fucking bitch," she whispered. "You fucking globe-trotting bitch. How is Rome this time of year, you cunt? You think Daddy would approve of that husband of yours? His brother is the assistant to Vito Ciancimino, isn't he? Mayor of Palermo? A mafia pawn."

The bloodstained woman spit on Valentina's forehead with disgust. Valentina flinched and moaned, trying to call out from beneath the leather glove.

"Is that what you support now? So determined to distance yourself from your father's legacy that you get in bed with mafia conspirators?"

Valentina tried to shake her head, blood trickling from her scalp.

The woman held up a gaudy-looking dagger between their faces.

"You see this? Know what this is? This is the type of dagger your father carried during the war. The type of dagger *my* father carried during the war. A ceremonial representation of the regime."

She twisted it in her hand to show off the details.

"The cross-guard is intended to evoke the crucifix, the sacrifice of Christ, who died for ours sins, just as our fathers sacrificed themselves for their family and country. Those men are God's chosen children. His warriors. Yet you ignored all that they gave. You bitch. *You bitch!*"

Valentina attempted to push the woman off, but as soon as she struggled, the woman thrust the blade into her torso, stabbing it up and under her ribcage.

Valentina gasped, her mouth filling with blood.

The woman pressed harder, deeper, scraping against the under part of her sternum. Soon she was up to her elbow inside Valentina, releasing a flood of gore that saturating the sheets.

"You have denied your family, Valentina Conti. You have denied your country. And your god. And for that, you die tonight."

ILLARIA TURNED OFF THE FAUCET, temporarily blinded by the water droplets running down her face. She reached for the hand towel near the light switch and brought the soft material against her skin, dabbing the moisture from her eyes.

"What shall we do tomorrow, then?" she called to Valentina as she hung the towel on its wall ring.

Opening the door, she was surprised to find the room had been reduced to darkness. Her impatient sister must have doused the lights and crawled into bed to pass out.

"Asleep already? Honestly, your tolerance has declined severely over the years."

She shrugged off her robe and slid into bed, pulling the satin sheets over her bare legs and nestling in. Even with the open window, the bed felt warm. Oddly warm.

"You're like a bloody heater, you know that?"

As her hand casually searched for her sister under the sheets, a pungent, metallic scent wafted into her nostrils. Instinctively, she jerked her head away as the odor intensified.

"Valentina?"

Her fingers had yet to locate her sister, but she felt something warm... and wet. And like a child sitting in a puddle, she was startled by the delayed sensation of moisture that now seemed to engulf her. The sheer curtains ruffled in the breeze, and as Illaria's eyes adjusted to the darkness, she saw the lunar glow from outside the window reflect off a wet pool of ichor slathered across the bedsheets.

Her arm extended beneath her pillow as the dreadful sensation of an unseen entity resonated throughout her body — the same feeling she'd had back in the kitchen prep area just before she was attacked. There was someone in the room with her. Someone who was not Valentina.

A gloved hand covered Illaria's mouth.

Then a croak of agony reverberated against the walls.

But the sound had not come from Illaria.

A woman, her gown crusted in a combination of fresh and dried blood, stood over her. In her dripping hand, she held the same terrible dagger the mysterious attacker had wielded — ornate, military in style.

Illaria held firm the handle of the chef's knife she had hid beneath the pillow, the recently sharpened blade now buried deep inside the bloodstained woman's chest.

The intruder fell to her side on the bed and Illaria had to roll out of the way to keep from being smothered. The woman's teeth gnashed as Illaria sprang from the bed and dashed out of the bedroom into the hallway. Illaria's shoulder slammed against the wall, ping-ponging her toward the living room as her momentum and balance tried to find an equi-librium.

The tears welling in her eyes partially blinded her, and she tripped over the ottoman. Looking back, she expected the woman to be hot on her heels — but there was no one there.

Taking advantage of her unexpected luck, she sprinted into the kitchen. The pairing knife was still in the sink, sticky with fruit juice from the dinner she'd made for her and Valentina. She scooped it up and spun around, prepared to defend herself. Using her forearm, she wiped the tears from her eyes to keep her sights clear, knowing any moment the woman would come around the corner, that sinister blade in her hand, ready to attack once more.

"Valentina!" Illaria screamed, though she already knew that the warm wetness that had covered the sheets could only have come from one place.

Trying to push her emotions aside, she did her best to focus on the inevitable face-off she was about to take part in, shaking her head as if she could discard the thought of her sister's death.

This isn't real, she thought.

This can't be real.

Why is this happening?

Her mind raced through a collage of memories: Seeing Valentina arrive at her apartment building. Giving her a giant hug. The two of them lying in bed together. Drinking wine. Slicing strawberries in the kitchen. Celebrating the death of her supposed attacker...

Illaria wasn't sure how much time had passed since she picked up the pairing knife. If it had been ten seconds or ten minutes, she wouldn't have known the difference.

Maybe the woman was dead. Maybe she'd bled out.

But Illaria was no fool. She wasn't about to let her guard down. No, the woman was still here. Somewhere. And sooner or later, she'd make her move. It was a game of reverse-chicken now. Both were waiting for the other to move, both standing still, knife in-hand preparing to strike as soon as the other grew impatient enough to come out from behind their security blanket.

"*Help!*" Illaria screamed.

She shouted out to anyone who might hear. Any of her neighbors living in the other apartments. Even if anyone heard her, however, by the time they made the trek over, whatever was about to happen would already have passed.

She looked around for anything she could add to her arsenal. Pulling open one of the kitchen drawers, she fished out a metal skewer. Unimpressed by the weight, she almost discarded it, but thought better when she saw the sharp barb at the tip and imagined shoving it into the woman's temple. She could almost hear the squelch of brain matter folding from the pressure, squeezing out of the skull in pink coils through the tiny hole.

She retched, covering the kitchen tile in a mess of red vomit, the result of strawberries, bile, and wine. Then, as she raised her head, she saw the woman was standing right in front of her. Like some unholy apparition, the woman leapt at her; the dagger slashing wildly, the chef's knife still lodged deep in her chest.

Illaria dove out of the way and sprinted for the door. She fumbled with the lock, undoing it just in time to slip out through the doorway as the dagger swiped at her once more.

Illaria screamed for help, her fists hammering against her neighbor's door. The bloodstained woman stumbled into the hallway behind her, the penetrating chef's knife jiggling with each step.

"*Open the door!*" Illaria screamed as she pounded.

The dagger jabbed at her, and Illaria grabbed the woman by the wrist and shoved her against the wall. She crumpled weakly, her strength fading, and the dagger toppled from her hand.

"*Someone help!*" Illaria screamed again.

The woman turned her attention to the chef's knife; her numbing hands fumbling at the grip. Illaria stooped down and stabbed both the pairing knife and metal skewer into the woman's side. The woman wailed in pain, trying to kick Illaria away, reaching for the dagger again. Illaria wrestled her hands back, then moved her focus to the chef's knife, attempting to yank it back out of the woman's chest. She could tell the blade was wedged between her ribs as she yanked the handle, twisting to find the exact grooves the metal had carved when it pierced through the woman's bones.

The woman clawed up at Illaria weakly, the remnants of her life seeping out onto the carpeted flooring of the apartment complex hallway. Then, as if she were suddenly injected with a dose of adrenaline, she backhanded Illaria across the face, sending her to the floor. She extracted the skewer from her side and plunged it deep into Illaria's thigh.

Illaria screamed, scooting away from the woman and pulling herself up against the wall. As she ran, she continued to call for help, praying at least one of the dozen sets of eyes that were surely watching through their peepholes would come to her aid.

Keeping her sights focused on the door at the opposite end of the hall, which led to a stairwell, she refused to look back over her shoulder. She accidentally jammed her index finger against the door as she grabbed the handle and thrust it down, but the pain didn't slow her pace. Down she ran, skipping every other step, then leaping over the last five to the side-walk below.

In the streetlamp's halo, she turned and saw the sagging silhouette of the bloodstained woman limping down the steps.

"My kind will always exist, Illaria." The woman's voice gurgled, like someone trying to speak with a mouthful of water. "No matter how hard people like you try to stamp us out, one of will always remain, ready to breed, ready to spread."

She came into the light, and Illaria thought she may have recognized her. *A guest from the resort?*

The woman fell to one knee on the sidewalk, the pairing knife jutting out from her side, the chef's knife still in her chest. She coughed out a spat of blood and wiped her chin, slinging the remnants away with flaccid fingers.

"We will light the world ablaze, scorch the ideas and beliefs of all others until everyone sees the truth, sees the world for what it can be, and follows in our fathers' footsteps."

The residents of the apartment complex began to appear at the top of the stairs, all of them staring dumbfounded at Illaria and the bloodstained woman.

Illaria looked up at her neighbors. She thought the terrified expressions that adorned their faces must have echoed the look Illaria had borne moments earlier. But not now. Her hands balled into fists. Her knees bent, ready to lunge forward and attack if the woman dared to rise again.

The woman smiled, her mouth stained red. "All it takes is angry, passionate words to spoken aloud, and for others to listen. And when enough people hear our sermons, when our numbers grow, that's when we start our *next* war for a better world."

Illaria crossed out of the streetlamp's light and approached her. She looked once more at her neighbors. With intention, each movement she made was slow and clear so that there would be no mistaking her actions. Her hand wrapped around the grip of the chef's knife and she gently twisted, finding the entry grooves in the woman's ribs. Then she removed the knife completely, letting the blood pour out across the sidewalk.

She leaned down, her eyes level with the woman's, seeing the realization of swiftly approaching demise in her face.

"What's your name?" Illaria asked.

The woman laughed through her nose, a spittle of blood oozing from each nostril. "Silvia Pasquale. Daughter of Silvano Frezza," she whispered.

Illaria wiped the bloody blade onto her bare thigh.

"No more talking for you, Silvia Pasquale."

Epilogue

Five months later.

Illaria entered the resort through the back door, as was customary for all employees of Terme del Paradiso. She placed her belongings in her locker and made her way to the kitchen by way of the lounge. She paused a moment, making eye contact with the newly hired bartender. He smiled and nodded at her, then went back to shaking up martinis for the well-dressed guests bellied up to the bar.

So much had changed in so short of time.

Yet so much remained the same.

In the kitchen, dinner service was winding down. Most of the guests had eaten and only a few tickets remained to be executed. Illaria went to the prep table, unspooling her leather knife roll bag, revealing the assortment of blades that her grandfather had gifted her a lifetime ago.

All chefs have a good scar or two, he had told her. *And they have a good story or two of how they received each of those scars.*

Illaria thought that perhaps the story of *her* scars was a bit more harrowing than most.

Removing the chef's knife from its sleeve, she set it on the cold metal surface of the table. Above all odds, she had gotten herself a job there at the resort, working under a renowned executive chef — something she knew she owed to her grandfather's kind and patient training. For a moment, she thought she could see his reflection gazing up at her along the sharp edge of the blade.

Today was the day she would honor his memory. Today was the day she would do her stage and prove to the chef that she was ready to rise to the next level. Cooking dishes alongside the true professionals. Crafting entrées from scratch. Every ingredient a meticulously selected component that would culminate into a finished piece of art. She had always wanted it. But now she *needed* it. She needed to put herself out there, willing to be judged, unafraid to receive the opinions of others in order to improve herself. One had to be open to criticism to reflect on one's own perspective.

Her grandfather had known that.

Her father had not.

And there was no question which of the two family members Illaria wanted to emulate.

The way the kitchen staff snapped to attention when the chef entered made her think of the military, the way she'd been told soldiers would straighten up when their drill instructor would enter the room.

Captain on deck. Was that the saying?

The sous chef led the way. The first line of defense. He introduced Illaria as if the chef was unaware of her existence until that very moment.

"This is Illaria Conti," he said, then stepped aside like some medieval herald now finished with his duties.

They had a large team, a necessity to handle a seven-day-a-week operation servicing the type of entitled clientele that frequented the resort, so it wasn't all that surprising that the chef, who certainly had a lot on his plate, may at the very least, not recall the name of every member of the team.

Illaria kept her eyes down, focusing on her knife roll, until the sound of the chef clearing his throat gave her the sign that he was ready to be acknowledged. Her gaze rose, and their eye line met. He was older than her by many years, the temples of his once jet black hair now graying. His embroidered chef's coat, free of a single blemish, was like the dress uniform of a royal general. All he was missing were the medals of valor.

To Illaria's surprise, he regarded her not with a grin, the way a debonair young man may attempt to charm a lady, but with a soft smile, like a parent pleased to be in the presence of their child for no other reason than to experience their company.

An overwhelming sense of ease coursed through her body.

His hands settled together behind his back and he leaned in ever so slightly from across the prep table toward her.

"Okay," he said. "Show me what you can do."

Afterword

I love hotels. You give me a book or film whose setting is some lavish resort or rustic mountain retreat, and my attention is all yours. Anything from *The Shining* (1980) to *The Inkeepers* (2011) to *Infinity Pool* (2023), you set a story in a hotel and my attention will be undivided. It was out of a desire to write a novel in such a setting that the initial seed for *Daughters Of Cruelty* was planted. The location isn't typically the first piece of the puzzle that surfaces when I'm planning out my books, but on this occasion, it very much was. I began thinking of what type of characters may exist there, and what events may occur within the resort's walls, which eventually lead me to the idea of making it a murder mystery. But not just any murder mystery. A giallo.

Though I was introduced to gialli many years ago in film school with notable examples like Dario Argento's *Deep Red* and *Tenebrae*, it wasn't until reading the enormously talented David Sodergren's novel *Dead Girl Blues* that my interest in the genre was revitalized. I spent a year going on what I called my "Gialli Journey" while writing this book, making a mere dent in the seemingly endless catalogue of giallo films, most of them from the 60s and 70s. I think I watched around sixty of them.

As with any mystery, it's not just about who did it. It's also why. So why did I write this novel? Well, my intent was to craft a story that could sit confidently alongside the work of Sergio Martino, Dario Argento, Mario Bava, and all the others who made contributions to the genre. I wanted to create something that felt both of the period that inspired it, and timelessly relevant. Also, as an added treat I threw in a few nods to other Italian sub-genres such as the poliziotteschi (Italian crime films inspired by American police thrillers such as *Dirty Harry* and *Serpico*), and mafia thrillers (because if you're going to set a story in 1970s Sicily, the mafia needs to be, at the very least, a background element). Full of red herrings, unsavory characters, shocking attacks, and eroticism, I hope *Daughters Of Cruelty* is one hell of an entertaining read. But you be the judge. It was certainly entertaining to write.

If you've enjoyed this novel and have never watched a giallo before, or have only watched a few, I hope this has sparked an interest in learning more about that underrated genre of Italian films. There are so many great ones out there. *The Fifth Cord, Amuck!, The Bird With The Crystal Plumage, Strip Nude For Your Killer, The Strange Vice of Mrs Wardh,* and *The Case Of The Bloody Iris* are all fantastic, just to name a few.

In parting, I'll leave you with a film review I was fortunate enough to write for the physical media release of Elio Gaeta's 1971 film, *No Mask For Breathing*. Vindictive Gems sent me a screener and it was an honor to contribute in even a minor way to the film's legacy.

NO MASK FOR BREATHING (1971)

Notorious Italian filmmaker Elio Gaeta's 1971 film, *No Mask For Breathing*, which recently found new life thanks to physical media distributor Vindictive Gems, is a luridly gratuitous, horror masterpiece. After being buried by its production company due to the overwhelmingly disturbing parallels between its subject matter and the real-life murder of Gaeta's model-turned-actress wife, Vittoria Gaeta, this exploitative thriller has finally been released over 40 years later.

The plot, which centers around an unhappily married couple on a Caribbean deep sea diving trip, is a jumbled collage of non-linear narrative, erotic dream sequences, and fourth-wall-breaking poetry readings, all of which somehow work together seamlessly in a sort of surrealist experience reserved only for the bravest auteurs.

George Perneau stars as Arnold, who enlists a local fisherman (played by frequent Gaeta collaborator Umberto Bonaro in a terrifyingly unhinged performance)to murder his wife and make it look like an accidental drowning. The scene-stealing heroine of this picture is, of course, Suzy Renzi, an actress who in 1971 was at the height of her fame, making it all the more head-scratchingly odd that the studio chose not to take the risk of releasing this fiendishly fun movie.

From the surprisingly humorous opening of Perneau and Renzi mid-argument on the deck of their yacht, to the white-knuckle climax featuring a moray eel with a, shall we call it *anal obsession?*, this lost treasure of Italian exploitation cinema is one for the speculative film books. And one I hope is finally given the deserved attention it was unjustly denied.

Though perhaps credit should be given to the film's production company for their self-control back then. Releasing a film about a man trying to murder his wife so soon after said film's director narrowly avoided prosecution for the death of his own spouse, would certainly have been in bad taste. However, now, so many years later, and with an emphasis on providing context, Vindictive Gems has given us what audiences were perhaps unready for back in 1971. *No Mask For Breathing* is a feverishly manic tale bathed in equal parts blood and salt water; a forgotten diamond, unearthed for a new generation of viewers, just as shocking and potent as the time in was made.

Available now from Vindictive Gems.

-L.J. Dougherty

L.J. DOUGHERTY IS A FREELANCE FILM CRITIC AND THE AUTHOR OF SEVERAL FICTION NOVELS INCLUDING BEASTS OF THE CALIBER LODGE.

Acknowledgments

To my wife, Tia, who is always willing to talk through a scene with me and share her creative insight.

To my son Declan — a light in my world while I write the darkness.

To my dear friend, Tim Taylor, for providing sound feedback and edit suggestions.

To the enormously talented Cameron Roubique, for always being excited to read my next book.

To Martina Bolognini for creating such beautiful cover art.

And to David Sodergren, for his generosity in penning the Introduction, and for sharing his giallo expertise while I researched this novel.

About the Author

L.J. Dougherty is the author of the Espionage Horror Series, which includes *Beasts of the Caliber Lodge*, *Primal Reserve* and *Blood Opus*. He is also the author of the survival-thriller *Woodhaven,* and the giallo *Daughters Of Cruelty.* He lives in California with his amazing wife, talented son, and goofy dog.

You can find L.J. on social media.
    On Twitter @LJ_Dougherty
    On Instagram @l.j.dougherty
    Or via email at LJDoughertyAuthor@gmail.com

NO
MASK
FOR
BREATHING
Are you ready to take
your last breath?
Directed by
Elio Gaeta
COMING TO CINEMAS
SUMMER 1971

"You'll need a shower after watching this film just to wash off all the sleaze."
—Rome Weekly
COLD GRAVE FOR A HOT HARLOT
The shocking new film by Elio Gaeta
In the name of the mother, the daughter and the holy whore...

Suzy Renzi

Umberto Bonaro

Vittoria Rosseni

le
puttane
sanguina
rosse

dirigida
por
Elio Gaeta

HENRY CHISOLM in
WET WALLS & BIG BOUNTIES
WYATT CAVE · DELIA PARKER · JOHN CAMERON
MATTHEW MITCHELL · SUZY RENZI and SCOTCH BONNETT
a film by ELIO GAETA   produced by CARL DROVER
MUGGINS GULCH STUDIOS   NIGHTMAREVISION   FILMED IN ULTRA·VIOLENT
WIDESCREEN - EASTWOODCOLOR

Non è solo sesso.
Un film di ELIO GAETA
VITA EROTICA
BARBARA CLEMMONS
PETER WALLEN

ORPHAN
SURVIVOR
WARRIOR
QUEEN

CARL DROVER presents
a film by ELIO GAETA
GEORGE PERNEAU - VANESSA TAMES

Attack
on
Deviltop

Daria Neri Armando Coy
Occhi di un ufficiale
prodotto e diretto da
ELIO GAETA